Shepherd's Warning

CW00530802

Shepherd's Warning

By Paul Melhuish

Copyright © Paul Melhuish 2024

The moral rights of the author have been asserted.

All rights reserved. No part of this publication may be reproduced, stored in or introduced into a retrieval system or transmitted in any form or by any means, electronic, mechanical, photocopying, recording or otherwise without prior written permission from the publisher.

This novel is entirely a work of fiction. Names, characters, places and incidents are either the product of the author's imagination or are used fictitiously, and any resemblance to any person or persons, living or dead, is entirely coincidental. No affiliation is implied or intended to any organisation or recognisable body mentioned within.

Published by Vulpine Press in the United Kingdom in 2024

ISBN: 978-1-83919-579-2

www.vulpine-press.com

To Dave

May Day

Simon knew that he was not alone in the wood.

Dawn cracked the horizon. The woodland around the lake should have been utterly deserted at this time of the morning and Simon should have been alone, but he wasn't.

Standing by the edge of the small, dark lake he suddenly felt- no, became aware- that he was being observed. Turning to look, his eyes picked out the pale shapes of the nearest tree trunks to him but anything beyond these was lost to the darkness. In his mind he knew that there were figures watching him in that darkness. A sense beyond mere sight and hearing identified the silent watchers, perceived their still vigil.

"Who's there?" he called out to the dark, soundless wood.

There came no reply but the feeling that he was not alone had continued, and became so acute that he decided to leave. Maybe, he reasoned, his imagination had got the better of him.

1

Simon pulled his wax jacket tighter around his body and navigated his way over branches and around tree trunks that were shadowed in the gloom.

Dawn crawled over the horizon like a slow burning lamp. The mess of branches, now back-lit by the glow of dawn in the East, gave some solace but Simon didn't stop to admire the enclosed scene. He just wanted to get out of this wood.

He intended to wait here until dawn broke – anything to be away from the village by the time *they* arrived – but he'd quietly freaked out. The lighter the sky became then more he convinced himself that the watchers had been a figment of his vivid imagination. He was a city boy now, not used to being in a wood at night. As he made his way along the edge the lake, Simon caught a glimpse of movement along the tight shore where the trunks encroached on the water. Had someone just darted out of sight, a clear foot to his left? His brain really was playing tricks on him. Now he thought he was being followed but that was impossible. He stopped.

How could they be following him without cracking over branches and rustling through foliage? This wood was wild and untended. You couldn't walk through Black Lake Wood without snapping twigs or brushing past branches that twanged back into place. He started again and thought- imagined- that he heard multiple footsteps keeping in time with his own, each step accompanied by a metallic *scihng, sching, sching.* Now he really was hearing things. He knew that sound. Knew it all too well.

Simon quickened his pace. The tales about the lake wood were abundant in the village. Ghost stories he'd heard at the bar of The Red Lion. He'd laughed at them but here, at dawn, alone in the countryside, they seemed plausible.

Ahead, Simon could see the stile and the field beyond, the incline reaching the horizon. He increased his speed. Behind him the *scihng, sching, sching* sound increased too to match his own footsteps.

The stile was now less than a metre away. He made for it and was out. Once in the open field, he stood on the other side of the fence and listened.

Nothing.

He sighed in relief. So, he did imagine it. Stupid twat. In his life he'd been to Beirut, New York, he'd even been to Kabul last year to lead a training programme. He'd navigated the London Underground when pissed nearly every weekend, and today he was scared of a fucking wood.

The light was really coming on now, making clear the details of the hedgerows to his left; the rows of green corn sprouts in the field behind him coloured the incline. The skies were cloudless. It was going to be a nice day.

Simon had intended to sit by the lake until full light, but his stupid imagination had scuppered that. He was going to then head east away from the village to that Café at the Hook Norton roundabout. Get a coffee, maybe a bacon

3

sandwich and waste as much time as possible. By the time he'd get back to Bracewell, the dancing should all be over and the Morris men would have left.

Simon looked to the hill and could see Bracewell church tower rising above like a finger pointing to the sky. He imagined that they'd all be there now to dance in the dawn. Strangely dressed people exiting from cars and gathering on the green. Accordions, fiddles and penny whistles tuning up.

Today was the day he'd been dreading. May the First. The day that the village of Bracewell ushered in the summer by dancing in the dawn. Morris Dancers from across the county came to Bracewell and took turns to dance in the road by the village green. Even the pub opened at 5:30am, and this was the only day of the year that you could get a pint at that time in the morning at The Red Lion.

Simon would have heard the music from his mum and dad's house where he was staying. Dad would have been struggling into on his jester's costume and Mum would have been putting on her clogs. No, he had to be out of it. With all the weird shit that had been happening over the last few weeks he couldn't face being anywhere near this folky madness.

And there was no way he was going to go and *watch* them. The pressure to don his brother's bells and baldric would be enormous. He used to do it when he was a kid, even into his teens. Callum had kept it up, right to the end but Simon was finished with that shit forever.

As he strode up the hill the sense that he wasn't alone returned like an unwanted rain cloud. Instinctively, he turned. Behind the green wooden fence that boarded the wood, five figures in white regarded him. What the hell was this?

He could see them as clear as day. Waiting behind the fence, all of them looking directly at him. Surprise, more than shock, rooted him to the spot. He studied them.

Each figure wore stained white shirts torn in places. Across their chests the criss-cross X of their baldrics denoted them as Morris men. If that wasn't enough the bell pads embracing their calves, pinching into their stained white socks, certainly gave them away. The *scihng, sching, sching* sound. The noise made by the bells of their bell-pads as they walked. Each man's face was shadowed by the brim of his top hat, garlanded with dead and wasted flowers. Even from here Simon could see the washed-out colours and broken straw of the boaters they wore.

Why the hell were they here? Why weren't they in the village getting ready to dance to 'Shepherd's Hay' or 'Nutting Girl' or any that old shit he used to dance to?

What's more they looked a mess. They didn't look like the well-turned-out Cotswold teams that would be dancing up on the green today. They looked like Morris men who'd crawled out of their graves.

5

He swallowed hard. This was a wind up. It had to be. He remembered the stories about the lake men, heard about their ghostly appearances. They all had. The way they stood with an almost solemn grace unnerved him. Their faces were still shadowed but each eye was trained on him.

Simon clung to the belief that this *was* a wind up, that these people were playing a trick on him, but that belief was shattered when, as one, they strode forwards and walked through the broken-down green fence as of it wasn't there. They passed through a solid object like ghosts. They made no sound in the wood but as they strode forwards now with rapid, deliberate steps their bells shook, creating that familiar rhythmic music. *Sching, sching, sching.*

He turned and ran, the sound of the bells following him. Daring to look back he saw them fan out behind him, and caught a glimpse of the deathly white eyes of the one nearest to him.

He crowned the hill and the sound of their bells ceased. Looking over the valley down to the woods there was no sign of them. They'd vanished. Like ghosts. He'd just seen ghosts. He'd actually seen ghosts. Not just ghosts but ghosts of the Black Lake men.

Screw this. He was going back to the village. He was going to march straight into The Red Lion and get himself a whiskey. A large one. Then he'd tell everyone what he'd seen and they'd all laugh, but he wouldn't care.

When Simon turned away, he realised they hadn't gone. The Morris men blocked his way, standing before him in a semi-circle. Simon let out a small cry when he looked into the face of the one directly before him. The face was black, and pure white eyeballs stared out from unblinking sockets. They closed in.

"What do you want?" he cried.

They said nothing, simply stared.

"What do you want?!" He screamed this time. Right on cue the music started from the village to the west. The first dance had begun. He recognised the tune. 'Cuckoo's Nest'. A Dance from Sherbourne.

As if satisfied that he was terrified- or perhaps they were waiting for the music to start to soundtrack his terror- the nearest Morris man produced an object from behind his back. He held it out by his bony, pale forefinger by the strap.

A set of Morris bells.

Simon stared at the bell pads. Seven, inch-wide bells fixed to a square of leather with a buckle to secure the bell pad to the calf. He recognised the object. Each bell was rusty, the leather of the bell pads cracked and rotten. These were his old bell pads.

'Where did you get those? How the hell…?'

He'd thrown these into the river Wye over ten years ago. They were supposed to be lost forever. Now five dead Morris men were holding them out to him. Through the cracks in his sanity, he realised the meaning, what they wanted from him. He also knew that they would appear to him again and again if he refused. Appear to him when he was alone. He knew what they were capable of. The last two months. The incidents. That had been just a warm up.

"I'll do it," he said quietly.

They stood, the bells still being offered. There was a symbolism to this act.

He snatched the bells from the Morris man, careful not to touch the hanging, corrupted flesh of the fingers.

"I'll do it!" he yelled into the dead face before him.

The Morris men tipped their hats to him and set off down the hill towards the woods, towards the lake. As they walked downhill their substance softened and they faded to nothing. Simon grimaced, began to shake as he clutched the bells, his mind unable to properly process what he'd just experienced.

The dance ended and applause caught his ear. The next tune started up. The whine of a fiddle and the breathy cry of the accordion.

'Constant Billy'. From Adderbury.

One

Five Years Later

"TALENTLESS WASTES

"SHIT YOU EMBRACE

"JUDGEMENT WIPES THE SMILE FROM YOUR FACE..."

Nathan took a step back as another slam-diver mounted the stage, and lunged into a heap in the middle of the mosh pit. Nick hit the double kick drums as the next verse kicked in. Nathan and Jake changed chords to bring in the pre-chorus. Nathan tightened his vocal cords to spit out the death-grunts.

"SUPERMARKET ZOMBIES

"CHICKEN SHIT CONFORMISTS

"MEAT FOR THE GRINDER

"FUCKED BY THE

"TALENT-FINDER..."

Nathan swore he could feel his head go purple as his vocal cords ruptured the chorus.

"BOW YOUR HEADS TO THE GODS OF SHIT BOW YOUR HEAD BEFORE THE GOOOOODDDSSS… OOFFFFF…SHHHHHIIIIIIITTTTTT!!!!!!!"

A slower break came in and he relaxed a little. His throat was fucked tonight and he was glad it was near the end of the set. He spat out a loose long hair as the same slam-diver mounted the stage again.

Wanker. He sometimes wished these people would just listen to the music rather than feel the need to show off. The back of the Oxenden Arms wasn't like the bigger venues where you couldn't get away with that shit. Places like the Boston Music room or the Borderline had banned slam-diving. The Oxenden was a tiny pub. The promoter was some teenager doing a business A-level, and all the bands playing here tonight were grateful just to get a gig when venues seemed to be closing down or turning into trendy gastropubs.

The place wasn't exactly packed but the usual faces were in attendance. Long-haired denim and leather metallers in Decapitated or Morbid Angel T-shirts. Nathan recognised them from the other bands playing tonight. A lot of punters were either in the bar, not even listening, or showing off like the slam diver. He noticed quite a few guys at the back. Normal looking older guys who'd come here for the music, just wanting to listen to some good metal as they clutched their pints.

The song came to an end and Nathan took long swig

from the bottle water bottle perched precariously on top of

the speaker next to him.

"Right, you fuckers. This is our last song. We are Inno-

cent Souls and you've been…average. As usual." The slam-

fiver raised his arms and screamed. Nathan rolled his eyes.

"Fuck off."

Three taps of the cymbal, and the last number kicked in

with a mean riff from the lead guitar before the drums

drowned it out. A mosh pit exploded in the little space be-

fore the stage and the few young, drunken nutters slammed

into each other. Nathan had given up caring if they hit the

monitors or not. He should be grateful. The previous band,

some hardcore outfit with a set of short songs, played to an

empty floor. Innocent Souls' form of sped-up death-metal

had at least got the punters going on a wet Sunday night.

Nathan's voice nearly gave out but he ended the song with

the refrain.

"CHOKE ON THE ACID CUM
COMMUNION FOR THE DUMB…"

***

"I just think we should change things, progress, y'know?"

After a few pints at the bar Jake, Nick and Nathan de-

cided to take the tube back to Raynes Park, to the flat he and

Jake had shared since coming down to London from Leeds

last year. Nick would drive the gear back to his place in Acton where they rehearsed.

It was Sunday, cold and wet. A typical English summer.

They crammed themselves and their instruments through the barriers, slamming their oyster cards onto the yellow reader and hurried down the steps to get the approaching tube before collapsing into an empty carriage.

/ who is Pete?

"I tell you what," said Pete, "the fucking sound was shit tonight. You could hardly hear the lead through the drums. When you did the decks at the Allatoch gig, Nathan, you had it just right."

"Yeah, but that was a bigger space," reasoned Nathan brushing his hand through his sweaty, red hair that hung in loose locks around his head. "Thing is, I don't wanna be just another fucking unreadable name on a bill of bands with fucking unreadable names. We're not gonna get anywhere like that."

"There was a mosh pit. What more do you fucking want, Nathan?" Jake was getting arsey. This seemed to happen a lot these days.

"I wanna do something that sticks out. Experiment. I wanna do something like Swans or Sunn-O."

Pete intervened. "Why not have a crack at folk-metal?"

They looked at Pete quizzically.

"You two are Morris dancers. You must know fiddle players and that."

Nathan grimaced. Then idea of fusing Morris with metal was something he'd spent his teenage years dreaming about until he realised that it would be a shit idea. It would sound horrible, like a lot of European folk metal that he wouldn't touch with a barge pole. He wanted to keep his Morris dancing and his metal band as separate entities. He knew Jake would like to do something folky, but Nathan wasn't interested. The tube pulled into Raynes Park and they exited. Nathan let them discuss it, his silence making it clear he wasn't interested in their project.

The tube arrived at their stop and they headed up stone steps to the surface. As fresh May rain poured from the sky, Nathans's phone buzzed.

"Hello?"

"Nathan. You massive ginger twat. Not forgotten what's happening in a couple of weeks, have you?"

"Hi Dad, what's on?"

"Bracewell Ale. Are you coming? The side needs you?"

"Is that still on? I thought they'd knocked it on the head years ago."

"No, Simon Weaver has taken it over from his brother. God rest is soul. Should be a good crack. Free beer. Come on, son, don't abandon your side."

"Yeah. Totally. We'll get the train up. I'll let you know times and that."

"Tell that lazy twat Jake to polish off his bells."

"Fuck off Moggy," Jake yelled down the phone.

He ended the call after telling dad about the gig, lying about how well he thought he'd do with his first round of exams next month, and promising to see them in Bracewell in two weeks' time.

"We should totally go," said Jake. "Their May Day bash was really good. We started drinking at seven, and went on until four."

"This is a whole weekend," said Nathan. "Not just the day. Great little pub there." He turned to Pete. "And it's haunted."

Pete was part of the paranormal society at uni. He suddenly became interested. "What, the pub?"

"No. the whole village. Never heard of the Black Lake Men? They appear every May Day."

"Then there's 'Shepherd's Warning'," added Jake.

"What's that?"

"It's a lost Morris dance. From Bracewell," explained Nathan.

They reached the door to the flat and he fumbled for his keys. The rain began to hammer down so they piled in once the door was open. In the lounge they dumped their things and instinctively Jake got some beers from the fridge. Nathan and Pete sank into the low sofas. Nathan cracked his can and drank deep.

Jake began rifling through the records, searching for something to put on. He grinned and took out 'Son of

Morris On'. The famous album of Adderbury Morris songs made in the seventies. It just seemed to fit the conversation.

"Yeah, 'Shepherd's Warning' is this lost Morris dance from eighteen-fucking –whatever. No one has danced it for ages because it's lost. The rumour is that every Morris side that has danced it has died afterwards. If you dance it, you'll die by before the next harvest is out. That's the legend."

"Yeah, because Morris dancers are all old fuckers," laughed Pete. "Apart from you two weirdos."

"No, seriously. It's a dance for six men, like most Cotswold style Morris dances. They reckon that all six men will die after dancing it because they're cursed. That's the story. Anyway, it's been lost. No one knows the tune or how to dance it."

"Thing is," said Jake with a broad grin on his face. "Our mate who's doing her Master's in history has been to Cecil Sharpe House. The folk history museum. She reckons she's found it."

Two

Nathan Moss had been Morris dancing since he could remember.

His father, Clive, and his mum, Marion, were folk enthusiasts and members of Wenley Moor Morris Dancers. He spent his childhood watching his parents dance at fêtes and days of dance, and had been taught to Morris dance as soon as he could walk.

Nathan was 24, and was one of the country's best Morris dancers. Unlike most sides comprised of middle aged and older men, his youth and years of practice meant that he could leap high and dance fast. Clive was Wenley Moor's 'Fool', the guy with the bladder that pissed about during the dances but he was a mean dancer himself.

Jake's mum and dad had been in the side as well, and he'd learnt to dance the same way as Nathan had: by parental indoctrination.

In his mid-teens Nathan had become cynical about Morris. Especially when he got into metal, but as he entered his late teens, he realised that Morris dancing provided opportunities to drink free beer. And that was good enough.

They'd danced at pubs, weddings, and fêtes, and if the venue didn't give them free beer, then someone always bought the side a few pints.

There were other reasons Nathan had stuck with the Morris in his late teens, though.

One day they'd done Manchester Day of Dance, and afterwards, he and Jake and a couple of other younger guys had gone clubbing still wearing their kit. They'd had so much attention from inebriated ladies when they'd rocked up in their smart shoes, ribbons, baldrics and straw hats. Sure, some people took the piss but he'd ended up snogging nine different women that night. That had never happened before.

By the time he was twenty, Nathan realised that he enjoyed Morris dancing more than he'd thought he would. He was good at it too. Apart from the social side there was nothing better than dancing a complicated dance well. Wenley Moor were a strong side now with a good reputation. Most of the guys were younger and good at it. A few of the older guys struggled with the leaping, but Nathan was the best dancer out of all of them, even if he said so himself. No point in being all self-effacing and humble. He was fucking good at what he did. Fact.

All in all, Nathan was grateful for his folky upbringing. As well as learning to dance, he'd learned to play a guitar and an accordion from the side's Squire, Derek. He'd stuck with the guitar and really practiced once he'd discovered metal. Nathan realised that metal and Morris weren't mutually exclusive. Many metal songs and folk songs were stories. Steeleye Span and Fairport Convention sang songs about lost sailors as did Iron Maiden and Alestorm. Both genres are littered with songs about war, murder, and the devil. A lot of folk music is even played in the same minor chords as metal.

Nathan had realised that both genres are room-clearers. If you had a dinner party for ordinary people who had a middle-of-the road taste in music (or wankers, as Nathan labelled them) then put on either metal or folk music and they'd soon get their coats on and fuck off home.

***

Nathan wound his way through the university building until he came to the library. Harris was at one of the low tables on the balcony overlooking the rows of books below. Sunlight, tempered by the tinted glass of the skylights above, brightly lit the library. Nathan rarely came into this place. He was in the second year of his Music Management degree, so didn't really need to engage with the academic, bookish side of learning.

Harris looked up, sensing Nathan's approach. She wore a corduroy jacket and faded grey jeans. Her hair was mousy brown, and she wore round Harry Potter specs. She was clever. Harris was the brightest person Nathan knew. She was far too clever to worry about the stuff her contemporaries, and even Nathan, worried about like relationships, pleasing other people or what her peers thought of her. Clothes were just a necessity for Harris as she was far too busy burrowing though books, trying to dig up obscure historical facts. Harris didn't really engage enough with the real world to bother dressing for it.

Nathan had met Harris when she had interviewed him for her dissertation on folk traditions. Harris was one for the few people Nathan knew who didn't take the piss out of the Morris, or show just a passing disinterest in it. Harris knew her folk traditions, and Nathan could talk to her about different Morris Dance traditions without having to endlessly explain it. Harris worked as a part-time lecturer here but as she didn't drink or like metal, so there were limits to their acquaintance.

Without preamble Harris held up her iPad. Across the screen he could see scrawled writing.

"I had a hell of a job finding this," Harris said, gesturing to the screen.

Nathan put his bag down with a thud, and sat heavily onto one of the low chairs.

"Is this it? Is this 'Shepherd's Warning?'"

"This is it. I went to Cecil Sharp House, and there aren't many dances from the Bracewell tradition. As you know, Cecil Sharp, was an associate of Vaughn-Williams, and went around the country in the early part of the twentieth century, visiting villages and rural areas to collect folk songs and dances. He transcribed them and they are all now kept at Cecil Sharp House."

"Yeah, I know all this Harris. Get to the point."

"Well, Cecil went to Bracewell in 1911 but none of the folk dances he collected there are kept at Cecil Sharp House. Don't you think that's strange?"

Nathan shrugged. "Maybe he left them on the train."

"But there was a wealth of historical evidence that Bracewell had its own traditions. There are historical accounts, such as diaries from clergymen, and even newspaper articles with photographs of Bracewell's famous May Day celebrations, and the Black Lake Morris men. This got me thinking…"

Nathan sat back in his chair. This was going to be a long one. He just wanted to look at the iPad, but Harris was in full flow now.

"Why wouldn't Cecil Sharpe file these dances away? He must have collected them. I spoke to one of the trustees who mentioned that a private collector had some of Cecil Sharp's documents. I visited this private collector in Oxford and…guess what?"

"What?"

"He had a transcript. The Bracewell dances. Only one of them. The paper scorched as if burnt, but here it is. He allowed me to photograph it."

He took the iPad and studied the photos, scrolling through as he went. On the paper he saw hand-drawn squiggles and notations. He also saw scorch marks on the paper. At the top of the piece of paper in old, joined up writing Cecil Sharpe had written:

Shepherd's Warning
A dance from Bracewell.

"Why's it burnt?"

Harris leaned back in his chair. "Odd, very odd. The private collector was the great grandson of a Clergyman called Lewis Watkins. Watkins was a friend of Cecil Sharpe's. Watkins rescued this from a fire."

"What, a house fire?"

"No. Cecil Sharpe was trying to burn his papers. According to his diaries, Lewis saw that Sharpe was burning them and went out and pulled them out of the fire. They argued but Sharpe wouldn't explain to Lewis why he was trying to burn the Bracewell dances. Odd. Why would Sharpe, a historian and man who devoted his life to preserving the folk traditions of this country be trying to destroy one of them?"

Three

No one really knows where Morris Dancing came from. Some think it originated in Africa and that the word Morris is a corruption of the word Moor, as in Moorish people. Moorish dancing. There is evidence that something very much like it originated in Tudor times when young men of the court would dance complex dances to woo ladies. Nathan had also heard that it came from farming communities where workers would use complicated footwork to shake the mud from their shoes, and this turned into a dance.

Nathan scrolled through the photographs Harris had taken, waiting for Jake to return from his grandfather's and arrive back at the flat. Jake had gone up to Leeds to visit the old geezer who had just come out of hospital.

Nathan had some problems reading the handwriting but the document was beginning to make sense. The scorched pages showed two rows of number fives in a straight line to the left of the page. The next page showed the numbers crossing over with each other and the page after that the dots made up a figure of eight. The dots were almost like footsteps denoting where the dancers should go, such as crossing past each other on page two, and the numbers were the figures. Nathan felt a slow buzz of excitement as the structure of the dance came together.

The door slammed shut and Jake bounded up the stairs like the lanky streak of piss that he was.

"I've got something to show you," he grinned.

"I've got something to show you as well," said Nathan holding the iPad out to him. Jake took it. "Harris emailed me these. She wasn't making it up when she said she'd found 'Shepherd's Warning'. I reckon I know what the figures are."

Jake frowned at the images as he wiped his finger across the screen. "Doesn't make a lot of sense to me. Whose handwriting is that? It's awful."

"Cecil Sharpe's"

"What, *the* Cecil Sharpe?"

Nathan recounted Harris's story of how he'd found the manuscripts in Oxford and how Cecil Sharpe had tried to burn them. The strange fact that a man who so loved English song and dance would try to destroy a newly discovered dance caused Jake to pull a deep frown.

"So, you know how in, say, the Adderbury tradition there are figures for a dance?" Nathan began.

"Yeah, half gip, process up, process down, hands round and hay. Yeah."

Nathan shot him a grumpy look. As children, Nathan's father had made them memorise the figures from each village's tradition.

"Well, this has a half gip in it. The figure where you cross over with the dancers opposite you. It also has a hay, the figure of eight movement we do in most dances. The dots in the figure of eight. That's what they mean. The rest of it I don't understand."

"Your dad'll understand it. Moggy spent a lot of time doing work for that EFDS." *Middlebury* *Shared Adda*

"The English Folk and Dance Society? Yeah, when we go up to Bracewell I'll get him to take a look at it. We'll have to work it out quick if we want to dance it at their weekend of Dance."

"Yeah, and I better make out a will, if you're supposed to die after dancing it. Maybe that's why old Cecil tried to burn it. To keep it safe from the general public."

"That did cross my mind," Nathan confessed. "But why go to the bother of transcribing it in the first place?"

"Do you think people really did die after dancing it?"

"Nah," said Nathan. "Some twat made it up for publicity. *Roll up, roll up, come and see the Morris men dance the Dance of Death.* People fell for that kind of thing back then. They didn't have the internet in eighteen whatever. Anyway, just think, no one has danced this for over a hundred years. We'll be the first side to dance it in Bracewell since probably the nineteenth century."

"We'll need the find the tune, find out what foot-work, what stepping it's danced in. Do you dance it using the

24

double-step like most Cotswold dances? I don't think we'll do it in time."

Jake had a point. There was a page of musical scores but as Nathan or Jake didn't read music despite playing music. It was no use to them. Sheila, their accordionist, read music and she might be able to play the tune.

Nathan lay the tablet down. He was sick of staring at it now. "What was this you had to show me?"

From his rucksack Jake produced a pale old cardboard shoe box. He pulled back the lid and nestling in a foam bed lay a handgun. It had a revolver mechanism and a small ring at the end of the handle. There were five bullets in the foam next to it.

"Fucking hell!" said Nathan taking the gun without asking. "This is your grandad's?"

"Yeah. That latest trip to the hospital scared him. Thinks he'd gonna die soon. He's fitter than me so that's bollocks but he's started giving stuff away. He gave his medals to me dad but this he gave to me. It's his Word War Two Webley. Pretty cool."

"Does it work?"

"He was shooting squirrels in the back garden with it last year. Thought I'd take it to college. Next time that gang of little shits that hang around Bargain Booze mouth off, I'll let off a couple of rounds."

"I wonder how many people this has killed?" Nathan grinned grimly.

"More than 'Shepherd's Warning' probably."

He raised the gun, pointed it at the kitchen sink and made a *pkhew* noise. Nathan held up the gun admiring it.

"Neat," he said.

Four

Some days the village of Bracewell looked like heaven on Earth, Simon thought as he drove the pick-up truck into the village.

The village was buried deep in the Oxfordshire countryside, which looked splendidly green this time of the year.

The lanes snaked their way through the tight hills. A sign bordered the village (Bracewell, Village of the year 2013, Please Drive Carefully), and a primary school to the left gave way to the village proper. The tower of the church presided over the village green, and was hemmed in by thatched limestone cottages, gardens blooming with multi-coloured perennials spilling over the picket fences and gates.

Simon came to the junction and stopped to let a tractor pass, the metal trailer brimming with hay. His own house, the house he shared with his mother and father, stood terraced by two other thatched, limestone properties and dead ahead stood The Red Lion pub at the foot of the hill. The road bent around the green and wound up the hill past the church. Simon looked down across the village. The little roofs and back gardens squashed against each other looked like some pre-industrial paradise on a day like this.

Following the lane, Simon left the village behind before arriving at the gate to Tithe Barn. A small meadow bordered by trees played host to the old stone barn. This time tomorrow they'd arrive for the Weekend of Dance and this field would be occupied by tents and campervans. He'd just come back from the brewery with four barrels of beer.

Blind Otter; a pale ale.

John's Dawn; a golden beer.

Early Spring and Late Summer; another pale and a tawny ale.

There were already four barrels that John, the Landlord, had supplied from The Red Lion but Simon was determined not to run out of beer like he did last year. Those boys from Wenley Moor Morris could drink like fish. Everything was nearly ready. His wife and sisters were sorting out the catering. There were two portaloos round the back, so all they had to do now was wait for them to arrive.

Stopping in front of the barn Simon climbed out and took in the peace of the afternoon. He loved this time of year. May Day had passed and the next one was eleven months away. He still couldn't face staying here for the first day of summer. Five years had passed and still it kept him awake at night. He struggled between one day believing he's imagined it and the next wondering if he'd really done enough to please them. He glanced towards the woods and swallowed hard. The Black Lake was down there. He never went out that way, even now.

Simon pulled down the tail gate of the truck. He hefted the barrels to the ground then went inside the barn to fetch the sack barrow. Pulling back the doors, he noticed that the tables had been set out. Lucy and Pat must have been up early to do this. Thin shafts of sun broke through the tiles above but the cool, if slightly musty, air in the old stone barn was a welcome relief to the mid-day sun.

Five years ago, he'd never have imagined coming back to this sort of life. He lived in London, he earned more money than most of the people in the village had seen in their lives, even the well-off commuters. Then his brother had become ill. Poor Callum was buried in the graveyard down the hill. Simon had done everything for Callum, for Mum and Dad as well, but it hadn't been enough. More was expected of him.

After Callum passed, he'd stayed. He'd lost his city job then he'd met Lucy. His mum and dad lived in the annexe and he and Lucy had the main house. He liked to think that Callum was looking down smiling at all of this. Of course, he'd never told anyone of what he'd seen that May morning. People just assumed he'd changed his mind after a long hard think. They assumed that Callum's death had made him take up the bells and baldric again. He'd not even told Lucy what really happened. However, there was something about this village. There always had been. Something odd, unseen, half whispered in the trees.

Maybe it was his paranoia.

Maybe it wasn't.

He brought the barrels into the barn and set them on their stands atop two long oak tables that had been there longer than he'd been alive. John would come up and tap the barrels later. He wasn't going to attempt it after blasting half of Northampton Morris Men with beer last year when he'd tried it. The Morris men and ladies could help themselves to as much beer as they wanted, but John still did a good trade. Especially last year when the football was on and a lot of the Morris men went down to watch England get hammered by the rest of the world.

He stood back to check the barrels were on their stands correctly and an uneasy silence fell over the barn. Simon was aware that he was no longer alone. He turned to see a pale, thin figure illuminated by the sun from outside standing just inside the door. The figure leaned on an old walking stick.

"Squire Wallace," said Simon somewhat relieved but not that relieved.

He'd not called him that for years. Mostly he just called him Wallace. Actually, mostly he avoided the miserable old sod. There were two aspects of Bracewell that gave him the creeps. One was the woods and the lake beyond the meadow here. The other was this guy.

Dark eyes scrutinised critically from under bushy eye brows seemingly made from grey wire. His bowler hat and waistcoat gave the impression of man who'd lived a hundred years ago. He was no longer Squire, or leader, of the side but he still put his penneth in if he though they weren't dancing well.

"This looks like it's going to be a good spread again this year, Simon." Wallace drawled in his thick Oxfordshire accent. "Should be a fair few coming then?"

"About forty sides and their families."

He drew closer to Simon, his stick hitting the ground with each footfall. The eyes still seemed to scrutinise critically. Simon felt a mixture of unease and annoyance. He'd never liked this man. He never smiled, was completely humourless and liked to boss people around. Even at his age. Why the hell was he here? He seldom ventured out of his rundown cottage on Banbury Lane. When he did, he came in to the pub, had a half, scowled and moaned that he couldn't smoke anymore, then went home. That was the limit of his adventures.

"Them lads from Wenley Moor comin'?"

"Yes. They always do."

Wallace held an uneasy silence then grunted. "That's all good then." He turned to leave. "The men from the lake will be pleased wi' that."

Simon froze to the spot. Had the old man just really said that? Had Simon imagined it or had he just made reference

31

to those walking corpses that had made their demands that May Day?

Wallace turned to leave.

"Wallace, wait." The old man stopped. "What do you know about the Black Lake men?"

"Well as much as you and a bit more besides. They spoke to you, all them years ago, didn't they. You didn't want to dance at Callum's funeral but they spoke to you and you did. You was never gonna dance the Morris again, you said. You was done with it. After you danced that jig, where was it, down in the Forest of Dean. When you hurled your bells into the water of the river Wye. You was done with it, you said. Now look at yer, they scared you so much you're back dancing with us again."

"What do they want?"

"They don't want nothing with you. All they wants is them lads at Wenley Moor to do a dance for 'em, is all."

"What dance?"

"'Shepherd's Warning.'"

Five

Paddington station had a bar that served alcohol from 9am, so Nathan and Jake took full advantage. The train to Banbury didn't leave until ten so they sank a couple of pints of Doom Bar before heading to the platform. As they left the bar, they hitched up their rucksacks containing, among other things, their Morris gear. The barman looked up when he heard the bells chinking as they left.

The train seemed to take ages to leave the station. Jake and Nathan sat in their window seats and Nathan took out the iPad again.

"You're not still looking at that bloody thing Harris sent you, are you?" moaned Jake. "You're obsessed with it."

"I won't have much chance to study it when we get to Bracewell, will I?"

He scrolled through but it didn't choose to reveal some vital clue. His dad would make sense of it, he was sure.

"So, when do you want do dance it?" asked Jake.

"If we can work out how it goes today then we can practice it Saturday Morning and dance it Sunday."

"Why can't we practice it tonight?"

"Because everyone will be pissed. I went to this last year. Friday you just set up your tent, go in the bar and hit the beer. People get their instruments out and someone might sing a song. Saturday, they take you on a bus tour of the villages around and dance at each village. We went to Hook Norton last year and danced at the brewery. Free beer. Sunday, in front of the church. That's when I want to do 'Shepherd's Warning'. I texted some of the other guys and they're up for it. Barry wanted a go but he dances like a horse on ecstasy so he's not doing it."

"Yeah, well try to be nice this time, eh? Warlock Morris still don't speak to us after The Forest of Dean weekend."

"But they did dance like they'd shat themselves."

"But there was no need to tell them that to their faces. Then there was that time you said Northampton were a bunch of wankers then found out two guys from Northampton were camped next to us. Awkward"

"I can't help being an arrogant bastard," Nathan grinned slyly.

"Maybe not, but if you can just keep your mouth shut, we'll be fine."

Nathan had known Jake since the age of ten. No one else except his father would get away with talking to him like this. Jake was practically family and Nathan was more grateful than he'd ever let on that the lanky streak of piss had moved down to London with him when he got his place at

North London Uni. He would have survived, made friends but it had been easier with Jake with him.

"What time's Moggy picking us up from the station?" said Jake.

"About twelve."

"This train better get a bloody move on then."

***

Clive Moss had been the fool for Wenley Moor Morris Men for forty years, after a brief stint as the Squire. He was in his sixties and his lank grey hair that ran down behind his ears as if he were a faded rock star. His goatee and moustache had gone grey too, but his lean physique subtracted ten years from his real age.

Nathan spotted the red antique camper van before he spotted his dad. Moggy bibbed the horn twice and drove over to the pick-up point. Nathan slid open the side door and they threw their rucksacks in.

"It's a couple of wankers!" he shouted jovially.

"Hi Dad."

"All right Moggy."

"You two stink of booze. Must have been drinking since nine, I think. You been to a Wetherspoons?"

"How's Mum?" Nathan said, ignoring his father's question. "She not coming down?"

"She'd lumbered with your sister's kids. I would have told Jenny where to shove it personally but you know what your mother's like. I'm just glad you won't be having any kids, Nathan. What with your tiny todger, and the fact that no woman would go near a lardy ginger fuck-wit like you in ten million years."

Jake was laughing and Nathan couldn't help grinning either. His father had joked with him like this ever since he could remember.

"Still playin' in that thrash band?" Moggy continued. "Innocent Smoothies, wasn't it. I looked you up on You Tube."

"What did you think?" asked Jake.

Moggy shrugged. "Fucking shite. Just noise."

Moggy drove the van into Banbury and bought them both lunch at a town centre pub. They sat by the window as tinny dance music hissed from the speakers, and the clamour of other diners filled the low-ceilinged room. They talked about the band, and their studies. Moggy gave them an update on how the side were doing without the two young dancers.

"We didn't even notice you'd left, to be honest," he quipped.

Then Nathan presented him with the iPad. Moggy put on his glasses to look at the screen.

After one very long minute he said, "Where the hell did you get this?"

"History student," was all Nathan would say. "What do you think?"

"Well, it gives the basic dance figures but no mention of the tune. Some of these dances have the music with them as well. You know, written down, but this hasn't. And I don't know what stepping they'd use."

"What about the figures then? There's a hay and a half gip."

"Yes…" said Moggy thoughtfully. "Remember what the Adderbury figures are?"

Of all the Morris Dance traditions, the ones from Adderbury were the most famous. When they were kids, Moggy was always testing them on which order they went in the dance.

"Half gip. Process up. Process down. Hands round and, lastly, the hay." Jake recited.

"Yeah, well this dance is like that except it's all backwards. Starts with a hay, then hands round, then process down, then process up then, lastly, half gip. Bloody weird. Like someone wanted to deliberately do a backwards Morris dance. Why would they do that?"

Jake frowned. "Maybe it's significant. Like, I dunno, saying the Lord's Prayer backwards in a satanic ritual. I mean, it is supposed to be a cursed dance."

"What, anyone who dances this, dies afterwards?" Moggy laughed and sipped his drink. "How do we know? And no one has danced this since this for over a century."

"Until now." Nathan's face was totally devoid of humour.

"Who's gonna dance this then?"

"We are. I emailed some of the other guys."

"Oh, are we now? And when are we going to do that?"

Nathan could feel irritation biting. Moggy was his father and could still infuriate him as all fathers could.

"Sunday."

"Well, sorry to disappoint you but don't think we are. There are three things we need to dance this dance. We need to know the figures."

"We've got them."

"We also need to know the stepping. What you actually do with your feet to get around. Is it single step or double step or something else? And lastly, we need the tune. See this page? It's musical notes but smudged and I see some of it's burned. I can't read these notes at all. I, nor any other musician, couldn't read this or play it. So, no one knows how the music goes. We're not going to find out how the tune goes before Sunday. Are we son?"

Nathan slouched back in his chair. "Shit."

Six

They'd arrived at two in the afternoon. The small meadow next to the barn was enclosed with trees and they picked their spot on the far side next to the wood.

While Jake and Nathan set their tents up, Moggy had a nap in his camper van. Other sides arrived and set up their tents too. Nathan and Jake went for a walk around the village. Bracewell hadn't changed in the last ten centuries of its existence, so Nathan hardly expected it to change in the one year since he'd last been here. They stopped for a pint in The Red Lion and Jake had asked Nathan why he was being a such a moody bastard.

"I'm not," Nathan had snapped defensively.

"You are. It's because you can't do that dance isn't it? I've known you long enough to know that you get all moody if you can't do what you want."

"No, I don't.' He knew full well that he did.

'You're such a prick. You really are."

By the time they'd arrived at the tents the other guys from Wenley Moor had arrived. There was Graham, a great big lumbering carpenter whose size limited how high he could get off the ground, and Wojtek, (pronounced Voiteck) a guy from Poland who'd come to England to study history. He'd previously danced traditional Polish dance and now spread his time between Wenley Moor Morris Men and a Polish folk-dance group. He was almost a good a dancer as Nathan. Wojtek was lean with dark, slightly curly dark hair. He exuded a cockiness that matched Nathan's own.

He was an annoying fucker.

He and Nathan engaged in a long running insult campaign which began when Wojtek pointed out that the extent of British culinary culture ran to fish and chips. Nathan had retorted by saying that all the Poles ate was cabbage. Nathan's insult name for him was Captain Cabbage. Wojtek's insult name for Nathan was G.C. (Ginger Cunt).

Moth (real name Maurice) was Moggy's age. He was a lean with a spiky shock of ginger-turning-to grey hair. He looked at the world from behind thick spectacles, and his wife, Sheila, a thin woman with very long grey hair, played the accordion for the side. Both of them were quiet people but both knew their folk music. Moth was fantastic on his feet even at his age and he must have been, what? Mid-sixties?

With these three guys and Nathan, Jake and Moggy that made six dancers that made up the side.

Nathan couldn't conceal his disappointment when he told them they wouldn't be doing 'Shepherd's Warning'.

"Are you telling me that no one in this fucking village knows the tune? One of the old men, maybe?" Wojtek's English was perfect but he still had an accent, especially when he dropped the F-bomb, which he did frequently,

"He's got a point. Maybe we should ask some of the old guys or maybe Simon Weaver knows it," said Graham.

Maybe someone did know the tune and the stepping to 'Shepherd's Warning'. He found his gloomy mood lifting at this new hope.

"If we all ask around, we might get lucky." He turned to Wojtek. "Well done, Captain Cabbage. I'll buy you a beer later."

"The beer's fucking free here, asshole."

They'd headed over to the tithe barn armed with their tankards and began drinking, catching up on each other's news and gossip from local Morris sides. A few of the other sides drifted in and gingerly conversations were exchanged until the beer loosened them up.

Once the sun had set the tithe barn came alive. Five fiddlers were knocking out a step-dance tune in the corner next to the beer kegs while several more fiddlers and accordionists at the other end of the room played 'Speed the Plough', a Morris tune. The music soared above the buzz of conversation and raucous laughter fuelled by the ale.

Nathan's tankard was empty but his limbs felt heavy with inebriation. He sat at a table with Jake and Wojtek. The babble of conversation decreased as his dad stood up to sing

'General Taylor' backed by Sheila on the accordion and Nathan felt a pair of eyes regarding him. The hall then fell silent as Moggy began to sing. He had a good voice but in folk circles that's wasn't that hard to achieve.

"Well General Taylor gained the day," Moggy sang.

"Walk him along, John, Carry him along," The hall rang back, their combined voices filling the barn.

"Well General Taylor he gained the day," Moggy attempted a falsetto on this line which made Nathan grin.

"Carry him to his bury'n ground," the hall chorused. Nathan still felt he was being watched.

He turned to see and old guy leaning on a stick by the doorway openly staring at him. The old man had dark eyes and bushy eyebrows. Nathan remembered dimly seeing him here last year but couldn't remember who he was. The man continued to stare.

"Tell me where you're stormy," Another falsetto to extend the last word.

"Walk him along, John, carry him along," Almost unconsciously Nathan joined with the chorus.

"Tell me where you're stormeee," Moggy sang.

"Carry him to his bury'n ground," The hall replied.

Nathan thought about going over and asking him what he wanted, but he felt it might be a bit rude getting up when his dad was singing. He stared back at the old man as the next verse kicked in. He wondered, as he sang back the refrain with everybody else, if maybe the old guy had dementia. Perhaps he, in his confusion, thought he recognised Nathan or maybe he'd had a thing for ginger boys in his younger days. Moggy sang on and finished the song before he got to the last verse.

"General Taylor he's dead and he's gone
Walk him along, John, Carry him along
Well General Taylor he's long dead and gone
Carry him to his bury'n ground."

The last line was delivered sombrely by the drunk singers in the hall. When Nathan looked again the old guy had gone. After the song people began to fill up their tankards and Nathan spotted Simon Weaver, Squire of Bracewell Morris side. Weaver went to fill up his own battered looking metal tankard so Nathan decided this would be a good time to talk to him about 'Shepherd's Warning'. A girl in her twenties from Charlbury Morris began playing 'Little Ball of Yarn' on her fiddle. The musicians around her joined in and Nathan decided now was the time to see him.

Pushing through the drinkers he Joined Weaver at the barrel of *John's Dawn,* the smooth golden ale they had on.

"Great do you've put on," Nathan hated small talk and this opening line made his awkwardness detector go into the red.

"Thanks. Wenley Moor, isn't it?" Weaver replied.

Simon Weaver had a thin face and Nathan thought he had a worried look about him. Rumour had it that he used to work in the city and made shit loads of money. He hated

43

Morris Dancing and had given up on it as a teenager but his brother, Callum, had loved it. Their parents were members of sixties folk rockers Weird Village (who's 1969 Album 'A Summer Pilgrimage to the Weird Village' went for six hundred quid on *Record Trader*. Nathan had it on CD*). Callum was allegedly a really good Morris dancer but had died young. About that time Simon returned to Bracewell and took up Morris dancing again and then became Squire of the side. He'd set up the Weekend of Dance a couple of years ago. Strange what a sibling's death will do. Nathan decided to get straight to the point.

"Listen. Does your side do any of the Bracewell Dances?"

Simon shook his head. "No, unfortunately not. They were all lost."

"Do you know any of the tunes?"

"No. Nothing survived. The original Bracewell side were wiped out in the First World War. It was only in the seventies when my parents moved here that we started the side up again. We just dance the usual traditions; Field Town, Adderbury, Bampton. It's a real shame nothing survived."

"I've found one."

"What? A Bracewell dance?"

Nathan couldn't help but notice the look of horror on Weaver's face. Maybe Nathan had misinterpreted it, perhaps it was just disbelief.

"Yes. I've only got the figures written down. I need to know what stepping they used and, more importantly, I need to know the tune."

Weaver frowned. Nathan sensed a real hesitation from this man.

"I don't know any of the tunes."

"Do you know anyone who might?"

Nathan saw Weaver swallow hard. He hesitated to speak, which Nathan thought strange, then words seem to tumble from his mouth, as if drawn out or expelled by some impetus which was not his own.

"The only one who might be able to help," he actually sighed at this point, "is that guy over there."

Nathan peered past a group of people to the see the old man who had been staring at him earlier.

"Squire Wallace. His father was in the original Bracewell Morris Men and he was squire of the second-generation Morris men set up by my parents. If anyone knows about the Bracewell tradition it's him." Simon took a sip of his pint. "What's the name of the dance you've found?"

Something made Nathan hesitate. He had the overwhelming feeling that she shouldn't tell Simon Weaver but fought it. "'Shepherd's Warning'."

Weaver had taken a mouthful of beer and Nathan thought he was going to spit it out over him. Instead, Weaver made a choking sound. If Weaver looked worried before he seemed positively spooked now.

45

"That one? There were nineteen Bracewell dances and you manage to find that one?"

"Yeah. The Dance of Death. Cool, isn't it?"

"Are you sure you want to dance it?"

Weaver was the first person he'd met who'd reacted like that, who appeared to believe that the dance was cursed. Nathan was surprised. None of the guys believed in the curse. Sheila, Moth's wife, had laughed and told him to make a will and even Moggy, who was a bit of a new age hippy at heart, had not seemed bothered by the prospect of dancing a cursed dance.

"Of course, I do," he retorted. "Don't tell me you believe all that you'll-die-before-next-harvest shit. That's just ploughboys talk and old wives' gossip from a hundred years ago."

"I'm not sure what I believe anymore."

Nathan hadn't quite registered what he'd said and would only later ponder Simon Weaver's odd comment. Fuelled by drink, Nathan sermonized.

"We live in a world of cause and effect. Science. The weather doesn't turn bad because you left a fucking pine cone in the porch. Hens don't stop laying because you haven't made a corn dolly or whatever and you don't die just because you do a Morris dance. Just think, no one had done a Bracewell dance in over a hundred years. We could make history this weekend."

46

Simon didn't engage with anything Nathan had said. Instead, he nodded over to the old man. "I don't give a fuck what you believe. I'm advising you not to dance this dance. If you insist, and I think you're mad." He nodded to the door. "Squire Wallace is just leaving."

Nathan saw the old man getting up, pushing up heavily from the chair so he rushed over.

"Squire Wallace?"

"Yes."

The old man regarded him from under those bushy eyebrows. He did not look friendly.

"My Name's Nathan Moss. With the Wenley Moor side."

"I know who you are."

"You do?" That would account for the staring. The old man must have seen the side dance last year and was trying to place him, so see if he remembered him. "Great. Look, I've-"

"I know what you want. You were expected. Come by my cottage tomorrow. Number 10 Banbury Lane. First light, if you can manage it. Before noon if you can't."

The old man walked off. Nathan watched him pass out of the door and into the night. Word spreads fast in this village, it seemed. The old man must have heard about their intention to dance and, who knows, maybe guessed Simon Weaver would point Nathan in his direction. They might be dancing 'Shepherd's Warning' after all. He refilled his tankard and went to tell the others.

***

Simon Weaver stood by the door of the barn in the darkness. He felt as if he was standing at the edge of a very high cliff. He shouldn't have pointed out Wallace to that young man but if he hadn't...

He sighed. He didn't want another visit from them. He never wanted to see them again.

When it all came down to it, he'd done what they'd wanted and perhaps they'd leave them alone.

***

Nathan stood looking into the trees, swaying. Everyone else had gone to bed. He could hear Graham snoring in his tent a few yards away. Behind him the hall was dark. A faint light was coming from inside his father's camper van parked across the grass a couple of metres away.

He'd drunk a lot more after his meeting with the old man. They'd been the last the leave the barn and now Nathan was contemplating trying to get into his tent. It would take a lot of skill and determination just to bend down let alone get the zip undone.

48

'Fuck it,' he said to himself. He needed a piss first. The portaloos seemed a long away across the small field, so he decided to go into the woods.

He stumbled forwards, feet catching on tree roots and he steadied himself on the trunks of trees as he went. He stopped beside a hazel tree, his vison swimming.

A soft mist drifted between the trunks. The moon above silvered the branches and leaves and he relived himself. As he looked, he saw what he thought were white trees standing close to him in a semi-circle, then soon realised they were people.

Five of them.

He was too drunk to register why five people would be standing watching him piss.

"Evening," he said, brain scrambling to identify the watchers. Were they wearing hats? He shook his head to try to clear his vision. They didn't respond.

"Don't fuckin' speak then. I don't give a shh…hit," he hiccupped. "What are you lot doing in kit? Don't need to be in kit until tomorrow."

The men wore top hats crowned with flowers and bal-drics crossed their chests. They had bells-pads around their calves. Wait, how the hell did they walk up to him without making any jangling noise? Nathan knew that when you had your bells on you could be heard miles away. You couldn't take a dump without someone hearing you.

He tried to see which side they were from. Their baldrics looked moth eaten but, in the light of the moon, they looked red in colour. Even in his pissed state he began to feel uneasy being stared at by these shadowed faces.

He zipped himself up. "Night night then." They still didn't reply. "Fuck yer then."

As he turned Nathan saw only trees. How far had he walked into this wood? The trees seemed to go on forever. He couldn't see his tent or his dad's camper van. What the hell was going on? He turned back to the Morris men to ask them what the fuck was going on but they'd disappeared. They'd not walked off, he would have heard them, but they'd simply disappeared.

Nathan turned back to see the light from Moggy's campervan and the shapes of tents on the grass so staggered back to the meadow.

Seven

Wallace's cottage lay down the hill from the church.

Nathan, Wojtek, and Jake arrived at the ironstone property, set back from the road and defended by a tangled garden of brambles and weeds. The cottage didn't look to be in the best condition. The window frame's white paint was grime-smeared and there were several cracks in the windows themselves. The front door was painted a faded green and was starting to rot around the bottom.

Nathan pushed the squeaky gate and led the others up the path between the stinging nettles. He walked boldly up to the door and knocked.

"You'd think he'd get someone to do the garden," said Jake.

"Age UK do my gran's garden. Perhaps this is a bit far out for them to come," said Nathan.

"Perhaps he's just fucking lazy," Wojtek chipped in.

"Probably best if you don't say too much, Wojtek," Nathan advised.

"Why, is he a UKIP racist asshole?"

"No, he probably doesn't like swearing," said Jake. "And as you can't manage to complete a sentence without the word 'fuck' in it…"

The door opened and Wallace greeted them with a half-smile that turned out to be more of the leer. He gestured for them to enter.

The living room was low-ceilinged, floored with worn carpet, and smelt of old tobacco. The ceiling had been yellowed by decades of smoke from, Nathan imagined, old woodbines. An ancient fireplace was surrounded by cracked white tiles that gaped out at them, and two low sofas sank up against the walls. By the bay window, Wallace took a seat at a desk cluttered with bank statements and letters. Nathan noticed a large accordion sitting on the floor. The three of them squeezed into one of the sofas because the other sofa was taken up by piles of clothes.

"Make yer selves comfortable. I'll get a brew on," said Wallace, and he went into the kitchen.

Tea might be just what he needed for his hangover. He'd drunk copious amounts of water and forced down a cooked breakfast in the barn. He had dim recollections of being in the woods at the end of the night and seeing some Morris men in kit. He was sure it wasn't a dream but the facts were hazy. He *must* have dreamed it. No one would be up at that time in their bells and baldrics.

Wallace returned with a pot and cups and set them down on the table.

"So, you wants to dance 'Shepherd's Warning'. Is that right?" Wallace stated in his thick Oxfordshire accent.

Nathan spoke up first. "We found some notes on the dance but there are gaps. Cecil Sharp collected all the Bracewell Dances and we've found one."

"I thought he'd destroyed them. Burnt them, I heard," drawled Wallace.

"How did you know that?"

"My dad told me and his dad told him. They said he was a funny bugger. Getting folks to sing, writing down the words. Some folks weren't happy that he was going about doing this."

"Is that why he burnt them? Out of respect for the traditions?"

"I don't know why he burned them. Something must have changed his mind about keeping them. So, 'Shepherd's Warning' was the only one that survived, eh? That doesn't surprise me. Anyhow, do you lot want to learn this bloody dance or not?"

"Yes. Of course, we do? Do you know it?" Jake said.

"My dad taught me all the Bracewell dances. Even 'Shepherd's Warning'. So, the thing about 'Shepherd's Warning' is that it's all backwards. Everything is done backwards."

"Yeah,' Nathan frowned. "You start with the hay where most Morris dances end with it. What about the stepping?"

Wallace stood up with an ease that seemed untypical of a man his age. "You ever done Badby Stepping? You do a double step twice then put your right foot across then your left. With this dance you *start* on the left foot, always the left foot, and cross left over right then do two sets of double steps."

Nimbly he demonstrated the foot work, crossing his feet first then hopping on the spot in a complex double step.

"I reckon I could do that,' said Nathan. Jake and Wojtek nodded in agreement. 'But what about the tune? Is that lost?"

"I told you," he replied with some irritation in his voice, reaching for his accordion. "My dad taught me all the Bracewell dances. That included the tune. This is how it goes."

The accordion took a sharp intake of breath as he handled it then exhaled with a high-pitched squeal. With his fingers flashing on the keys, he began to play 'Shepherd's Warning'.

Nathan listened carefully. The tune used minor chords mainly and had a dour, almost sad refrain. The hooks of the A music sounded like a funeral procession but jogged along at speed. The B music, or chorus, kept the sombre mood and Nathan had an image flash in his mind. Of a man drowning and reaching through the water for light that faded the deeper he sank.

"Try the footwork," ordered Wallace. The guys stood up and practiced the complex stepping. In a couple of minutes, they'd accomplished it.

"I reckon we could do it," said Nathan. "If you teach our musician the tune."

"One question," said Wojtek. "If you know this tune and this dance why haven't taught your own side how to dance it?"

Wallace squinted. "Foreign, eh? Comes to something when we have to import foreigners to dance our own traditions because English men don't want to no more."

"Yeah, yeah, yeah," Nathan changed the line of conversation. "But he has a point. Why haven't you revived the Bracewell traditions?"

He shrugged. "My dad came back from World War One with shellshock. Never danced again. The rest was killed. It wasn't till the end of the sixties when Bruce Weaver and his missis moved here that they wanted to start Morris dancing. They was in that rock band wot did Morris tunes. I never held with that really. Also, it didn't seem right, strangers dancing the dances my dad and his dad danced so I kept quiet about it. Taught them the Abberbury and Fieldtown traditions. Now you turn up with a scrap of paper eager to dance the Dance of Death."

"So, you'll let us dance it but not 'strangers' who've lived here for fifty years?" Jake put in.

Wallace scrutinized them in that disconcerting way. "Some things is just right," he said after a long pause. "I'm not long for this world and I'd like to see it danced in Bracewell before I go. And you lads was born into the Morris, I

55

can tell. Well, most of you." He shot a glance at Wojtek. "And I don't see as it'll matter that you ain't from theses parts dancing it if *I* plays the tune."

"You'll play it for us?"

"Yep. We'll get over the barn and go through it just after lunch and again in the morning. You can dance it last thing Sunday." He leaned forwards with slightly crazy look in his eyes. "On the Sabbath."

He laughed and Nathan wondered if he was slightly mad. Or maybe dementia was kicking in.

"And what about the curse?" said Wojtek smiling wryly. "Does that bother you?"

"What? That if you dance this you die before harvest is done? Nobody's danced this since 1890, and the last bunch to dance this didn't drop dead before harvest."

"No?"

"No. They died *as* they danced it."

***

"Some folks thinks ghosts is just impressions left. Echoes like. Others thinks they is spirits trapped in this world, unable to get to the other side."

Wallace didn't look at them as he spoke. All three of them sat, eager to hear the story Wallace was about to tell.

"This was passed down to me from my dad and that was passed down from his dad. On May Day in Bracewell, it's tradition, as you know, for the Morris to get up before dawn and dance in the first sunrise of summer. Most Oxford sides dance up at Oxford on May Morning and some of the other sides over the border in Northamptonshire dance up at Brackley on May morning."

"We dance in Wenley Square on May Morning," Wojtek interrupted. "It was fucking cold this year I tell you."

Nathan shot him a glance to shut him up so that Wallace could continue his story.

"Since Bruce Weaver came, he started up the tradition again. Back when the Morris was danced in villages, we danced in the May Day here. That's what they used to do in the nineteenth century. Back then, according to my dad, the Bracewell side was made up of twelve men. Six of them were the best dancers in Oxfordshire. The best dancer was called Billy Brice. He could leap twice as high as any man and they danced fast. Like you blokes do. They were probably like you blokes. Young, headstrong, wanting to show off. The spring of eighteen ninety was when it happened.

'The spring was slow to come. There was snow in April and everything was froze. The lake out by the woods had been frozen for months. Black lake. So come May Day it was still ice. So, Billy Brice and the side put on their bells and baldrics and went out to dance in the May morning in front of the church as they always had. However, Billy had the bright idea of doing the first dance down in the woods, actually on the lake. He persuaded four of the side to go with him but one of them, Will Sykes, didn't want to do it. He said that the ice would have thawed and all that leaping and dancing on it would crack the ice. So only five men danced it, not six as is usual."

"Let me guess," interrupted Nathan. "They all drowned."

Wallace looked genuinely put out that his story was interrupted.

"As you know, there need to be six dancers for the Bracewell traditions. Will Sykes thought they might not do it without him but they did. They danced 'Shepherd's Warning' on the ice at dawn with the whole village watching. They danced it without slipping over until they got to the half gip then Billy leapt as high as he could. As he landed the ice cracked. It spread out like an old spider's web and in they plunged into the freezing water.

"No one thought the lake was that deep, six-foot at most, but they ended up under the ice where it was thicker…"

Wallace let the story hang.

***

"So where did this idea that you die if you dance 'Shepherd's Warning' from," Nathan asked.

"Well, one of the ones who didn't dance it, Will Sykes, went off his head. Gave up working and lived in a shack in the woods. A year later the fathers and uncles of the five lost boys were going to dance it as a memorial to them on May morning. Sykes told them all that April that if they would dance it, they would all die as their sons had. He was mad but he had such a way of talking that he made them believe it. He got religion in the end and went around the villages preaching but always came back each May Day and hung crosses around the trees in Black Lake Wood."

"What has this got to do with ghosts?" asked Wojtek. "You started talking about ghosts."

"Because they've been seen. Out in the woods. A couple of campers came into The Red Lion one night back in the fifties saying they'd seen them in the wood. Morris Men in kit. They've been seen more recently. On May Day."

Suddenly Nathan began to question if he had been dreaming last night.

"By whom?"

"Simon Weaver. Came up the hill screaming that he'd seen five dead Morris men out Black Lake way. He don't like to talk about it, though. Get a few drinks inside him. He'll might tell you the story."

Eight

Nathan's hangover melted into the warm fuzz of drunkenness as the village tour progressed. The six Wendle Moor Morris dancers dominated the back seat of the coach like the bad kids at school. The bus toured five villages in all and the plan was that at each village the dancers would get off, have a drink and a dance at a pub then get on again to go to the next village. Wojtek passed round a hip flask which initially took the edge off, but at the first village- Hook Norton- they danced in the town square and outside the old brewery. Nathan had a couple of pints at the brewery which eradicated the hangover by the time came for their first dance.

They danced 'Nutting Girl' then 'Beaux of London City', a stick dance. With each dance Nathan sweated out some of the alcohol. They boarded the bus and entertained the drinkers in The Fox at Sibford Gower, before moving off to Wardington, then Bledstoe. Moggy played the fool in his battered top hat and long coat. Looking like a Victorian chimney sweep, he battered their arses with his bladder on a stick and generally tried to put them off.

Wenley Moor shared the spots with four other sides which gave the guys a break and a chance to get a beer when they weren't dancing. At Wroxborough they danced in the middle of the road, at a junction in the village next to an old pub with nicotine-stained walls and ceiling which reminded Nathan of Wallace's house. Nathan and the others leaned on the wall clutching pints, and he looked past the shabby boarder side from Highcross shuffling through one of their own made-up dances and spotted Simon Weaver standing on his own.

Nathan wanted to talk to him and ask him about his May Day experience but it didn't seem right just to go up and ask him what happened here with all this going on. However, he might not get another chance. They had a hog roast on when they got back to Bracewell and Simon would be busy with arranging all that. Nathan might not get another opportunity to talk to him all weekend, and he felt he needed to clarify with Weaver what he'd seen last night.

"Now ladies and Gentlemen," announced Moggy as the Highcross side shuffled off, "It it's my great displeasure to announce that these bunch of show-offs from Wenley Moor are going to dazzle you with their footwork as they dance 'Lads a Bunchum'. Feel free to throw stones at the ginger one."

The moment was lost. Wojtek handed the sticks round and they put down their pints on the pavement to take their places in the road. There weren't many non-Morris folk watching. A couple had come out from the cottage with their young child to watch and an old lady was standing by her triangular walker clapping along.

After two notes from the accordion, they strode round in a circle singing,

"Oh dear mother what a fool I've been,
Six young fellers came a courting me,
Five were blind but the other couldn't see,
Oh dear mother what a fool I've been…"

As they verse ended, they came back into formation, two lines of three, and, as one, clashed sticks. The dance had begun.

They double stepped through the figures, passing each other right shoulders in a half-gip, tunefully hitting sticks at each chorus, the end two dancers dancing into the middle of the set then the rear two dancers doing the same. After hitting sticks again, single handed this time, they each linked hands and practically threw each other in a circle before hitting sticks again but this time overhead.

During the final figure, (the hay, a figure of eight movement), Nathan felt his calf muscles begin to ache. A sign he was getting tired. He leapt into place and turned to let Jake, his partner opposite, hit his stick as he thrust it over his head. The dance ended and they paraded around in a circle and gave their sticks to Graham who was the right-hand man at the top of the set. He held his arms out as they piled up the sticks. Nathan raised his hat to the couple with the kid.

He knew they'd danced this well by the hearty applause they received from the other sides. Sweating, Nathan picked up his pint and downed it in one.

"Another?" said Jake.

"Fuck it. Why not."

Northampton took the performance spot and didn't even try to follow that. They opted for a simple hanky dance from Wyvern called 'Jubilee'.

***

The final spot was in a pub car park on the edge of Banbury with precisely no one watching except other sides. They cut that spot short and, feeling pretty oiled now after having two pints in every village, Nathan boarded the bus back to Bracewell.

As they pulled up outside The Red Lion, Wallace was waiting for them, wearing his scowl with his accordion hanging around his neck like the mariner's albatross.

"We doing this dance then?" he barked at them as they got off. "Or are you lot too pissed?"

"We're okay," Nathan spoke for all of them. "Let's do it."

"Right. Well, go up the barn then."

Simon Weaver was the last off the bus and saw them trudging up the hill while everyone else went into the pub for a late lunch.

"Where are you going?" he called out.

"Practice." Wallace called back.

"Practice what?"

Wallace stopped and Nathan saw an almost sinister grin spread over his face. "Surprise."

Nathan also noticed the expression of concern, of dark caution in Weaver's eyes.

**

"So, are we cursed now?" asked Wojtek barely suppressing a snigger.

They'd gone through 'Shepherd's Warning' twice and nailed it. They'd had the hall to themselves but knew people would be drifting up soon from the pub. As no one had danced if for over a hundred years any incorrect footing wouldn't be picked up. Wallace, who's played the dour tune, was happy with how it looked.

"No son," replied Wallace. "The curse starts when you dance it in kit in front of other people."

"Like we're going to do tomorrow," said Moggy.

"Like you're going to do tomorrow."

64

Nine

Nathan didn't believe you could die just from dancing. Reality didn't work that way. Nathan believed that reality was based on scientific lines. Cause and effect. His way of thinking was absolute, and not only did it carry him through the rehearsals for 'Shepherd's Warning', it fed into the thinking of the other guys. After they'd danced it a second time on the Sunday morning, Jake pretended to have a heart attack, which Moggy didn't think was that funny as his doctor had prescribed him Amlodipine for his high blood pressure just that week.

Nathan and Jake had picked up the strange backwards dance quicker than the others. Wojtek and Moggy took to it, but Graham's footwork was messy - he always seemed to struggle with leaping about due to his size. Moth seemed almost reluctant to do this dance and fucked it up a couple of times, which was strange for him as he was such a nimble-footed geezer.

Nathan didn't know Moth that well. He knew Moth had religious beliefs because he was a church warden but he wasn't very evangelical. Nathan considered taking him aside and asking him what was wrong, but he wasn't a bloody counsellor. Moth was going to do the dance and that was all that mattered. Besides, if he believed in God, wouldn't God protect him from any curse? Not that Nathan believed in God. The stories and myths pertaining to Christianity were so absurd that he had little respect for any seemingly intelligent person who believed them.

Today they would dance 'Shepherd's Warning' for the first time in over a hundred years and make Morris history. They would prove this curse was bullshit and kill two birds with one stone. That was all that was going to happen.

People filtered in for breakfast, and Nathan decided to get a shower in the shower block at the sports centre down at the village. He'd drunk a lot last night again and could smell the fermented booze excreting from his skin. After that, some breakfast would be needed to soak up the remaining booze, then he'd put on his kit and they'd do what they'd come here to do.

Give the supernatural the middle finger.

***

Simon Weaver's relief that the weekend had gone so well was tempered by a nagging fear. Wallace was up to something and he didn't trust the old Squire one bit. Apart from being moody and unpleasant, the man was part of this village through and through. He knew about the Black Lake

Morris Men and…he was somehow *part of it all*. At first, he'd thought maybe Wallace was a victim, like himself. He'd said as much they day before yesterday when they were in the barn. Now Simon felt as if Wallace wasn't just fearful of them, but was in league with them. He didn't fear them like Simon did. Yesterday the Wenley Moor men had visited him in his cottage.

Simon had a very bad feeling about this but what could he do? He'd warned that Nathan guy, but he wasn't going to listen. Maybe some of the others would. Moggy for instance. His internal circle of fear led him to the same logical conclusion. The Black Lake men wanted them to dance this. If he interfered…

So why did they want Wenley Moor to dance 'Shepherd's Warning'? The last side to have danced this had been the Black Lake Morris Men. They'd died doing it. So why did the dead want the living to perform the Dance of Death? Just for old time's sake? Weaver knew more there was more to it than that.

Screw it. He couldn't stop it. It was out of his hands now.

***

Breakfast had merged into lunch and many of the Morris sides had already packed up to leave. Each side would do a final dance on the road in front of the church. This would be their show dance and after most people had drifted off.

In front of the pub and along the road to the church all the sides had gathered. In the midday sun they stood out in their different coloured attire and the whole thing looked like a psychedelic minstrel gathering. Bells, baldrics, ribbons and flowered hats were sound-tracked by the noise from fiddles and squeeze boxes turning up. Simon saw the Wenley Moor side, in their red baldrics crossed over their chests, standing with Wallace who had his squeeze box slung about his neck.

Moggy was the compere for each side and announced the first dancers to perform. Northampton Morris Men kicked off with 'Broad Cupid', a dance from the village of Badby just over the Northamptonshire boarder.

Next came Highcross Ladies Border Side, a new Northamptonshire side performing their own invented border dance called 'Lady Grey'. This was a stick dance which a lot of whooping and yelling. They wore grey and red dresses and their faces were painted red. At Moggy's next announcement Simon's guts tightened.

"And now, the Wenley Moor Morris Men will dance for you a dance that has not been danced here since eighteen ninety. Some call it the Dance of Death, others call it the cursed Dance. Legend says that if any side dances this dance, they will die before harvest is out, so if someone can give us the number of a good funeral director and tell our wives and mistresses we love them, we would appreciate it. Laydeeezzz and genteeelmen…we give you…'Shepherd's Warning!'"

Simon watched as the five Morris men took their places. Five dancers only, just as the Blake Lake Morris had danced with only five all those years ago. The echo made Simon uneasy.

Wallace began to play the tune, a dour and almost threatening piece.

They leapt into life, first with a left-over-right foot cross, then danced up and down the column in a double step. The dance began with a hay, the figure of eight movement where the dancers weave around each other.

Simon wondered how they'd learned this so quickly as they'd only practiced twice. They demonstrated more poise and energy than any of the other sides. As one they left the ground and clutched hands to swing each other round, first one way, then the other way. Their hankies hit the air above as one, as if white flames were licking the sky.

Next came a half gip, where the dancers passed right shoulders and leapt into the air at the side of the road before returning back to formation.

Simon looked at the other sides. Most of them stood around, some watching intently, most just half-watched, engaged in conversations. The Northampton men were sitting on the wall with the church rising up behind them on the elevated ground. Simon perhaps expected a black cloud to drift over –the sky was clear blue – or the church bell to start tolling ominously.

The tune rolled out across the village. A staccato fugue of the A music. The higher-pitched, but no less sinister, whine of the B music. Their feet skipped over the dry tarmac of the road, their white handkerchiefs licked the sky, and suddenly it was all over. The dance ended as it had begun, with the six men in two columns crossing their feet before coming to a standstill at the final, low chord from the squeezebox.

5 or 6?

A moment's silence then the applause. They'd danced well and the keenest observers gave the loudest applause. It was over. They'd danced the dance and nothing had happened.

Movement in the churchyard caught his eye. Simon could feel all the colour drain from his face.

Five of them stood, each behind a grave selected almost at random in the churchyard. The colours were the same and the hats were rimmed with flowers, but they'd lost their air of decay and death. They were too far away for him to pick out facial details but they stood there, looking down, unnoticed by the crowd below. The Black Lake Morris Men were watching. No one else seemed to notice them. They were just another Morris side in kit waiting to dance but Simon knew who they were.

As Wenley Moor Morris walked round in a circle doffing hats to their audience, the Black Lake Morris Men left their places standing on the graves and walked calmly around to the far side of the church.

70

Simon looked to the crowd to see if anyone else had noticed them. No one had. Only Wallace, who was looking up to where they had been, smiling to himself.

Ten

Nathan, Graham, Moggy, Wojtek, Jake, and Moth cele-
brated with a beer. They were the last ones at the bar of The
Red Lion and they forensically picked through the nuances
of their performance. The took the piss out of Graham for
being slow-footed but generally congratulated each other on
a dance well danced and theorized how to improve on it next
time.

Nathan could have happily sat at the bar of this lovely
old pub all afternoon and sank pint after pint of Old Hooky,
but they had a train to catch. Moggy was beginning to give
him that tired look that meant he wanted to leave so they
placed their empties on the bar and left, trudging up the hill
to the campsite.

They'd pulled down their tents that morning and loaded
them into Moggy's Jeep. Nathan quickly changed out his
Morris kit and he slipped on a pair of shorts and a T shirt,
relived to be out of the long-sleeved shirt and knee-high
socks on such a hot day. Wojtek was going back with Moth
to Leeds, but Graham said he'd come with Moggy in the

truck and keep him company once Jake and Nathan had been dropped off at the station.

Nathan felt a knot of homesickness when Moggy asked Moth and Wojtek if they were up for the York Day of Dance next week.

"I'm back in Poland for two weeks but after that," said Wojtek.

"Well, bloody lot of use you are, seeing as it's next week," laughed Moggy.

Nathan missed the dancing out, the banter. He missed home and family but was torn; his studies, the band, and everything else in his life was in London. He made a mental note to tell Moggy he'd come up and visit him and Mum next month.

They said their goodbyes and climbed into the truck. Moggy twisted the ignition key. Nothing happened.

"That's strange," he said. He twisted it again and the truck jumped into life. "I'll have to keep an eye on that."

Nathan took one last look at Bracewell before they drove out of it. Simon Weaver was walking up the hill when they passed. They waved but he didn't wave back but just looked at them like they were some strange lifeform.

"Miserable sod," said Graham who was sitting in the front seat.

"Maybe he found that pile of puke on the cricket pitch from last night," laughed Jake.

They left Bracewell behind and were soon travelling through the country lanes to the main road when the truck began to judder.

"For fuck's sake," cursed Moggy. "I had this serviced last week."

The truck began to lose power on a single-track road, before finally dying as Moggy steered it into a passing place on the right-hand side.

On the other side of the road tall oak trees swayed in the breeze over a small brook obscured by greenery. Moggy gunned the engine but it was dead.

"Pop the hood," said Graham unclipping his seat belt. "I'll take a look."

Graham opened the door but quickly shut it again as a tractor appeared from behind, roaring along the road towing a large trailer of hay bales.

The tractor stopped beside the truck and the driver leaned out of his cab.

"You guys all right?" asked the young man wearing a flat cap. Nathan got the impression he was a bit of a Young Farmer. They'd danced at enough Young Farmer's dos for him to know the type. If this guy could tow the truck to Banbury, they might even make the train.

Graham got out and squeezed past the front wheel of the tractor.

"I'm just going to look at the engine, mate. Might just be misfiring or something."

Graham wasn't an engineer but he knew more about engines than any of the others did. Nathan watched as Graham stepped out in front of the tractor to get round to the front of the truck.

He didn't even see it coming.

No one heard the sound of the engine approaching from the top of the hill. Nathan just saw the flash of a black Audi's bonnet, and Graham temporarily framed against it before it hit him, smashing into the front of the tractor with Graham caught between.

Graham didn't stand a chance.

Eleven

"Don't you say it. Don't you say a fucking word."

In the heavy silence of the flat, Nathan knew what Jake was thinking. No one had mentioned it in the aftermath of Graham's death, when they were standing on that road waiting for the police to arrive, trying not to look at the human mess between the Audi and the tractor. Blood and flesh amalgamated to smashed machine and chassis parts.

After signing statements, they took the train back to London in shocked silence. The Police were going to tell Graham's widow, Alison, the bad news. Once back at the flat, Jake and Nathan simply didn't know what to do, or how to process what they'd seen. They consoled each other that at least it had been quick. The next few days were a blur. Nathan had an essay to complete, so had thrown himself into that.

Nearly two weeks had passed and they'd gone up for the funeral. Graham was well known among the Morris community in the North but his side had been asked by Alison, to dance his favourite dance at the funeral. According to Moggy his favourite had been 'Valentine', a Fieldtown

76

Morris dance. It had been the first one he'd learned to dance when he'd first began dancing with this old side, Leeds Morris Men.

The chapel had been packed with men and women in strange costumes and flowered hats, but this only added to the sadness of the day.

Nathan hadn't known Graham that well but had danced with him many times. He reflected on how close you become to the people you dance with. You symbiotically join with them and take cues from them to match footwork and movement. That alone brings you closer to the guys you dance with in a way that mere conversation couldn't. It was a bit like being on a football team, you worked together to make something. Graham had been a bit slow due to his size but he knew the moves and the footwork.

After the eulogy from Graham's father, from Moggy and then a short speech by the vicar they carried they coffin outside. Even the pall bearers were Morris men, and Nathan almost smiled at the absurd sight of four blokes in straw hats with flowers in them carrying a coffin to the grave.

As the coffin was laid into the ground in Wenley's seemingly vast necropolis – Nathan could see nothing but headstones for metres in every direction – Sheila disrupted the silence with the jaunty tune to 'Valentine' and the Wenley Men naturally fell into set. All the men who had danced 'Shepherd's Warning' that day danced. Graham was replaced by a guy called Trevor from Ickley Morris whose footwork, Nathan thought, was terrible.

Nathan began to feel the knot of emotion pull at his guts, tears pricking the backs of his eyeballs as they danced in honour of their fallen friend.

At the wake none of them felt like drinking, except Graham's wife who, at the third glass of chardonnay, started to cry hysterically. She was in her mid-thirties and a widow already, poor cow. That wasn't something you just got over. Her sister and mother tried to console her in the corner of the pub.

Before they left, she came over and thanked them for dancing, saying that it meant a lot, and Nathan felt his eyeball prickle again. Before he lost control and started crying himself, they got out of there.

Nathan took in a lung full of cold summer air, and the shock that had numbed him for the last two weeks began to subside.

He went back home and stayed in his own bed that night before meeting Jake at the station and returning to normal life.

Innocent Souls had a gig on Sunday at The Oak. Until today he'd thought of cancelling it, but now he felt a sort of release. As if burying Graham had drawn a line under the whole shitty event. On the way home, the train passed through Banbury and the rest of the ride reminded them of the journey back after his death that day.

Now as they sat in the flat, the air clear, Nathan was able to tell what Jake was thinking.

"I wasn't thinking anything," replied Jake.

"Bollocks. You were thinking about the curse. All the dancers die before harvest has finished."

"It was an accident. I don't believe it any more than you do, Nathan."

"Good. But you were thinking about it."

"Well, of course I was. Didn't it cross your mind?"

"No!" Nathan was on his feet, almost shouting. "Because he was hit by a car. It was a bloody accident. Nothing more."

"Right."

"Right!"

He sat down and switched the TV on. Some mindless property show was on.

"Fuck this," said Nathan. "I need a drink."

Twelve

"TAKE THE PLATTER
TO THE MASTER
LAY IT AT HIS FEET
FEEL THE SHOCK
THE EMEMIES MOCK
AS THE SEVERED HEAD BEGINS TO SPEEEEEEE-
AAAAAK!!!"

Nathan began to feel his throat give out at the last death grunt. He reached for his pint at the foot of the amp and took a swig before they started the next number.

For a Sunday night there was a fair few punters in at The Oak. A thin topless guy with a crew cut joined the mosh pit as he fingered the opening chords to 'Bow Your Heads to the Gods of Shit'. Jake joined on the bass and the drums thundered in. There were five of them in the mosh pit to start, and they were soon joined by another three long-haired guys. Two girls stood at the edge, nervously pushing back against the frenzied thrash of fists that were being thrust in their direction.

Most of the time they played there was no mosh pit at all, just an empty space at the front and a circle of either bored looking punters or nodding heads.

"BRAINLESS PILES OF HUMAN MEAT

BEFORE THE SCREEN TO GAZE AT THE REPEAT

OF THIS ROTTING CORPSE THIS FUCKING FARCE

FEEDYOU CATTLE WITH THE SHIT FROM ITS ARSE..."

This felt good. Nathan felt the grief being beaten out of his system. He was waking up, coming out of the coma of bereavement. Before him the moshers fell back as one, momentarily stopping while a couple of guys who had fallen were helped to their feet by those who had just helped to push them over.

"HOPEFUL WASTELS KEPT IN LINE

EAGER FOR THE SLAUGHTER TIME..."

The mosh pit surged forwards and encroached into the stage. The topless guy pushed backwards onto the monitor before flying up furiously into the fray, fists out like lightning, as he piled back into the group of hairy guys.

Nathan's pint had been knocked over and a dark spread of Doom Bar was inching out across the small stage. Now he had nothing to wet his throat before numbers and he'd need to be careful not to slip. Nothing funnier than members of an extreme metal band slipping on their arses during a show.

"BOW YOUR HEADS
BOW YOUR HEADS
BOW YOUR HEADS TO THE GODS OF
SHIIIIIIITTT!"

The puddle of beer spread around the amp to this left. The squat, black box was old and the leads were hanging out of the back, plugged in and taped together. Nathan wondered how the landlord let them get away with such shoddy electrical workmanship. Nathan re-focused. There was a solo coming up and he'd need to play the second part.

"UP BEFORE THE BOLT-GUN JUDGEMENT
I'M SINGING THIS SHIT FOR MY DAUGHTER
WON'T WASH THIS THE FAT DECIDER
YOUR HEAD IS ON THE BLOCK."

The puddle lapped at his feet, spanning at the way to eh back of the amp. The amp was shaking, as it always did, and he noticed the electric leads loosening.

If they came out, he would be in for a nasty shock. Nathan tried to catch the eye of the guy on the sound desk at the back of the room but he had his head down, monitoring the sound, sliding the controls up and down. He looked back. The lead had shaken out of its socket by half an inch.

"BOW YOUR HEADS
BOW YOUR HEADS
BOW YOUR HEADS TO THE GODS OF
SHIIIIIIITTT!"

He screamed the chorus, maintained the lead riffs, then cut in with this solo.

Shit!

The lead had come out another half inch. If he didn't do something he'd get fucking electrocuted. Like the intonation of some lying serpent, the thought came into his mind: all dead by harvest time. Was he going to be the next one? Was this the curse working its magic?

No, that was bullshit. However, he was going to get electrocuted if he didn't act fast but there was no way he was stopping mid-song. Not with an appreciative crowd and an insane mosh pit in front of them.

With the solo finished he looked to the lead again. It was holding. They had about 30 seconds before the song ended and he could stick it back then. As he leaned forwards, the bass-growl of his vocals shook the speaker again and the head of the lead dropped as it prepared to fall out.

Before him a thin stream of beer made its way towards Jake's feet. Bloody hell, did the curse want to take them both out?

Towards the back of the room, Nathan's gaze was drawn to a flash of white. In a split second he saw, or thought he saw, the white shirt and straw hat of a Morris man passing along the back of the room. He looked again and there was nothing. Not only was he about to be electrocuted, he was now seeing things.

The lead was ready to drop.

Right, fuck this, he thought. I'm just going to stop, get off the stage and let the sparks fly. His fingers left the guitar strings. The lead dropped right into the puddle. He tensed ready for the shock but the lead rolled away. The sound went from the amp.

So much for the fucking curse, he inwardly laughed.

A burst of movement to his right caught his attention. The topless thin guy had mounted the small stage. In his right hand, Nathan saw a stout, serrated blade of a hunting knife. The guy thrust it forwards in machine-like movements, puncturing Jake's gut repeatedly. Nathan froze as he watched the guy raise the knife as Jake fell back against the drums. He brought it down in a swift, targeted ark into Jake's chest. Once. Twice. Three times.

Panicking people were starting to run out of the hall. The drummer slid out from behind his kit. The room filled with the shriek of feedback from Jake's guitar.

The logical realization flashed through his mind. If he didn't do something, he would he next. The topless guy's eyes were dead, no emotion. He was like a machine.

Nathan lifted his guitar over his head, unstrapping himself from its embrace. He raised it by the neck and brought the full weight of its body down on the attacker's neck. He fell forwards onto Jake, stunned but not unconscious. Two of the hairy blokes from the mosh pit grabbed him and put him to the floor.

"Jake. Jake!"

He took hold of Jake by the shoulders. Blood was pumping from the wounds mingling with the spilt beer on the floor. Nathan knew he was gone, but he didn't want to believe it. His eyes were focused on nothing. He was limp and not breathing.

"Someone call a *fucking* ambulance!" Nathan screamed above the whine of feedback.

Thirteen

Wojtek shouldered the rifle as the boar came into the view. The stunted form of the black pig trotted across the clearing, and he had a perfect shot. It would be a head shot, a clean kill. He hoped, anyway. Most of the time it wasn't and either the dog would finish the pig off or he'd have to fire at point blank range as it writhed on the floor squealing having been hit in the legs or flank.

He flicked off the safety catch and got ready to fire. He was about to pull the trigger when a second black shape trotted into the clearing. This one was smaller and it was joined by a second and a third.

The piglets followed their mother across the clearing. He counted five of them. Wojtek upended the gun and flicked the safety back on. He wasn't going to kill the mother and let the piglets fend for themselves. They'd starve to death. None of the hunters would do that, not even his uncle, Pan Christof, and that guy was one fucking asshole. Especially when he was on the vodka, which he was most mornings.

Wojtek had looked forward to coming home to Poland, but his father had given him a list of jobs almost as soon as he'd walked through the door. Tomorrow they were tiling Panni Hella's new bathroom, and the day after he was chopping wood for the winter. Since being in England, Wojtek had got used to doing fuck all except drink and English folk dance. He worked as a translator sometimes when he wasn't studying but that wasn't real work. That was just sitting in an office on a phone. You didn't even break sweat translating. He'd be breaking sweat in the next few weeks, now he was home.

Wojtek's family lived in Rawa Mazowiecka, a small town thirty kilometres from Warsaw. His father had built a large house right next to the forest where he could hunt and get firewood. His father was a builder, good with his hands, all his family were and he'd worked hard to get the money to send Wojtek to England to study. He planned to stay there. There was fuck all here in Rava and he could earn more money in England than in Poland. Lots of Poles came to England because there were fuck all opportunities here. Sometimes he wanted his country would get its shit together and be like England. Leave the arseholes at the EU like Britain had, pull its ass out of the past and make some fucking money.

One thing the Poles had that the Brits didn't was a sense of cultural identity. Last year, at his sister's wedding, they had to shut the disco up because they were all singing 'Szla

Dzieweczka'. He could never imagine that happening at an English wedding. The English all sing John Barleycorn or whatever. Wojtek had learned to play the accordion when he was eight and everyone here knew Polish dancing. In England it was practically dead. Only a tiny minority did Morris dancing, and the rest of the country took the piss out of them for doing it. England was stabbing itself in the balls. Culturally anyway.

He stood up. The pigs had passed. Wojtek turned the 360 to see where the others were. He'd left at dawn with his dad, Joreck, Pan Christroph, his brother Meireck, Pan Kubosh and Pan Bartoz. They were just behind him and now they were gone.

He thought about shouting out their names but if they had spotted another boar, and were about to shoot, he'd scare it off.

A faint mist hung around the straight boughs of the pines. Foliage sprouted green around the feet of the trees. A bird called out once, but the wood seemed eerily silent. The path was some metres back and Pan Christoph's truck was parked there. Maybe they'd gone back. Christoph would be needing a shot of vodka by now, he reckoned. He could do with one himself.

Turning, he made his way back to the path by stepping noisily through the foliage. The bird that had been singing took flight. After five minutes he expected to find the path

88

but he didn't. He'd only managed to get further into the wood.

He looked around for familiar markers but there were only trees here. They all looked the fucking same.

Shit.

He turned back and headed for the clearing where he'd seen the pigs but a sound made him stop. A harsh clink of metal echoed through the woods followed by another.

"You are shitting me."

He stopped, listened. To his right he heard the *shing-shing* of the bells that the English dancers wear, that *he* wore. He must be imagining it. Who the hell would be wearing bell-pads in Poland?

An explosion of feathers broke the silence as a group of pigeons burst into the air, startled by something.

As the sound of their wing-beats faded he could hear the bells again, a rhythm created by the small bells with each footstep. They were heading his way.

A sudden fear settled over him. Was he losing his mind? After seeing Graham die like that had he gone a bit mad? The sound stopped, and a wisp of mist passed between the trees. As it cleared, he spotted a figure standing a few feet way. It wasn't his father or any of his uncles. This man was wearing a top hat ringed with what looked like dead flowers. This chest was crossed with a dark red baldric. Wojtek could see the bell-pads at his knees, the bells dark and rusted.

The man's shirt was grey, eaten away in places, but it was the face that freaked him out. Pale, like a dead man, but hollow eyes, black with no expression. Behind him stood four other Morris men.

What the fuck was this? Someone playing a joke? Wojtek knew it wasn't. There was something unearthly about this.

'Who the fuck are you?' he said, instinctively speaking English to them. 'Why are you here?'

Unanswering, they continued to stare.

"Fucking speak, you assholes. What do you want?"

Wojtek thought about running but imagined just getting lost with these assholes following him, trying to freak him out. Instead, he tried another tactic. He raised the rifle and aimed it at them. To his left he heard movement in the undergrowth. He dismissed it. Probably a bird of a squirrel. He had weirder things to worry about.

"You guys better start talking or I start firing." He flicked the safety off.

As one they moved forwards. Their bells made sound but he couldn't hear the branches breaking beneath their feet as they moved. With disbelief, Wojtek saw that their feet passed though the undergrowth leaving it undisturbed. He looked up to see the first one walk through a tree trunk like it wasn't there.

He fired. The bullet passed through the Morris man and hit the bough of the tree he'd just walked through.

As soon as the shot erupted, the creature to his left rushed towards him. Panicked by the shot, the boar blundered out of the undergrowth and launched itself at Wojtek. He felt the full weight of the creature, a hefty male, pile into him and felt the horns catch on his stomach.

Wojtek crashed to the floor and the creature ran over him, back hoof sinking into his right eye before smashing into the undergrowth and making its exit.

Fuck. That was close. He tried to get up but a paralyzing coldness prevented him. He looked down his body.

"Oh, no. Fuck. Shit. *Hollerah. Strentner.*"

His intestines were trailing across the forest floor, caught in the horns of the boar as it had gored him. Steam rose from them in the cold morning and blood seemed to be gushing out from somewhere. If his father and uncles didn't find him soon...

The Morris men stood over him, looking down and he realised.

The curse. That dance. Fucking 'Shepherd's Warning'. It was all true. These *dooch,* these ghosts had come to let him know.

"Hollerah," he groaned as he got weaker. *"Hollerah."*

Fourteen

The last thing Nathan wanted to do was dance in this fucking graveyard again but here he was. They ran through 'Vandals of Hammerwitch', an 8 man stick dance and Jake's favourite.

He tied the grief in a knot in his throat to stop the tears coming but above all the overwhelming sense that this was just wrong infected the very air around them.

The man who's stabbed Jake to death that night was known to mental health services. Some fucking schizo off his meds and hearing voices. He'd never been seen at any of their gigs before or at any gigs, at the Oxenham Arms or even the Boston Music Rooms. For some reason, known only to himself he'd targeted Jake. He'd been taken back to the nut house where, Nathan hoped, the bastard would rot.

The dance finished to no applause and they headed away from the grave along with the other mourners.

Jake had been pronounced dead at the scene. Nathan had solemnly helped his parents clear out his room. They hung his bells and Baldrick up in his room which, no doubt, they'd keep as a shrine to him, their boy who had been taken from them at such a tender age. He was twenty-four. Sometimes Nathan wished there was a god so he'd have someone to blame. Nathan had kept the gun. His parents hadn't asked for it so he didn't mention it.

He'd got changed with his dad and Steve then they climbed into the van and drove to the pub. The Keystone was one of those soulless establishments with a big screen and a miniscule selection of real ales. Nathan didn't feel like ale today. He had a large whiskey.

The three of them sat in the corner.

Moggy raised his pint. "To Jake."

"To Jake," they echoed.

Steve took a slug of his cider, while Nathan downed the whiskey in one.

His dad gave him a reproachful look. "Steady on."

"What do you mean?"

"You don't want to drown your sorrows is all I'm saying."

"I'll poison my sorrows with this shit if I like."

"Yeah, well,' Moth piped up. 'Don't you think it's a bit strange?"

"No," snarled Nathan. "No, I fucking don't."

"I think it's a bit funny. You know what it said, all six dead by next harvest."

"Which harvest? The potato harvest? The tomato harvest? The end of the next tax year? It's. Bull. Shit! Jake was murdered by a schizophrenic. There's a lot of mad cunts about these days. Graham was hit by a car. That's it."

"Yeah, well, I had a bad feeling about dancing that dance," said Moth.

"Then why didn't you say anything?"

"Would you have listened?"

Moggy cut between them. "Right, shut it you two. This won't bring Jake back. Here," he slipped Nathan a tenner, "Get another dram but make it a single this time. I don't want you coming back the house arseholed."

As Nathan went to the bar, Moggy's phone started to ring.

"If this is bloody work. I told them I was at a funeral."

He got up to answer it, passing out of the front door and lighting a fag as he did so.

Moth was religious. He believed in the irrational. It was part of his nature to see connections in these deaths. Perhaps it was part of everyone's nature. He was right about one thing. The deaths were bloody weird. Nathan did as his dad had said and got a single only. As he got served Moggy came back into the pub.

"That was Mum," he said. "She just had a call from Poland, from the brother. Nathan, I can't believe it. Wojtek. He's dead."

Fifteen

Clive Moss hadn't always been a Morris dancer.

As a young man he'd embraced religion and had gone around the country with his brethren in a van to towns and villages every weekend to preach in market squares, village greens, anywhere really. Anywhere where people would listen. The Lightbringers, they called themselves. Clive hadn't done any of the preaching, he'd just played the guitar. He'd been baptized as an adult. They'd been preaching at a folk festival in Derby when he'd met Marion. He'd talked to her about Jesus and she'd taught him how to double step. She was open and friendly, funny and full of life. He'd joined her Morris side to try to convert them to Jesus, secretly to spend more time with her, but had ended up enjoying the dancing and playing guitar.

The crunch had come when Pastor Andy warned him that dancing was not Christian, and that God would punish him for it. That didn't make sense. God made man to dance. David danced in the Bible, there was a hymn about Jesus dancing. Maybe God didn't like that awful music his son made in his thrash band because it sounded so evil, but Clive couldn't understand a God who hated the Morris. Clive left the church and married Marion.

He'd not thought about Pastor Andy and the Lightbringers for years. He'd not been to church for that long but since leaving Bracewell he'd thought about them a lot. He'd even taken his Bible from the loft and read parts of it. Since Dancing 'Shepherd's Warning' he'd felt uneasy. That was before Graham had died. Now two more of the dancers had died and a darkness hung over him. He thought about Pastor Andy's warning more and more. Perhaps he had been right. Perhaps, hidden beneath the bells and the flowers, something ancient and evil had laid waiting.

Nathan had got drunk when he'd heard about the Polish lad. Moggy had left them too it and come home. Nathan got in a few hours later and went straight to bed, hardly able to walk. Now the sun had set and Moggy looked down the garden. The door was open and soft light from the living room cast shadows down the path.

Marion was out. Ironically, she'd started going to church about two years ago and was over at Jake's mother's house consoling her after the funeral.

If the curse had been true then how did it work? How could this evil power reach all the way to Poland? Moggy didn't know. He could hardly believe that he was thinking this way again after so long but something in his soul told him that his fate was sealed. He'd danced the Dance of Death and there was no going back.

His own death he could face but not his son. Sure, Moggy hoped for grandchildren. What father didn't? But any father would move heaven and earth to save his kids. Nathan was so young with so much to learn. Once he sorted himself out, he'd make a life for himself. Clive knew that. Now his future was under threat.

Inevitability. It manifested itself in many ways. He stood up, walked slowly to the patio door. Inevitability had manifested itself here tonight.

"So," he said as much to himself as to his visitors, "You're here."

***

Nathan felt his stomach lurch and wondered if he should get up and try and make himself sick. With consciousness came the reminder of the awful situation he was in. Wojtek dead. He had to admit that the curse was real. This was too much to be just a coincidence. Three of them had died. Three.

And it was all his fault.

No. that was bullshit. *Bullshit!*

***

They waited at the end of the garden. The light colours from the pale, dead flowers in their hats were just blobs in the gloom. Their dark eyes seemed like mere tears in pale white cloth. These were the Black Lake Morris Men. They were here for him.

Clive thought he'd seen them when they'd danced the Dance of Death up in Bracewell. As they'd finished the dance, Moggy had seen Simon Weaver looking up at the church. He'd followed the man's gaze and saw five figures. Five Morris men standing in the shadow of the church. He'd blinked and they were gone.

They waited in a semi-circle regarding him silently. How they got here he didn't know. They were spirits. Ghosts of dead men. How they got here was not important. Why they were here *was* important.

He faced them. "I know why you fellers are here."

Right on cue he felt a burning pain in his arm radiating up his armpit. His chest became heavy, like there was a baby sat on it. Like Nathan used to sit on him when he was a toddler. Moggy felt his breathing become heavier, more laboured. He didn't have long. A minute? Maybe less.

"Right. I have something to say before I go. We're all six of us Morris men. Ain't we?" They didn't move. "Ain't we?" He said with more urgency.

The pain was increasing. With a movement barely perceptible the man in the middle nodded his head in acknowledgement.

"Good. Now listen…"

***

98

Nathan slid from the bed and into an upright position. He still had his clothes on, his Morris kit in fact. He'd not changed from the funeral. He'd had the good sense to take his bells off, at least. They were in the bag at the end of the bed unceremoniously dumped.

A sudden light caused him to look to the window. Cloud which had obscured the moon now passed causing the white satellite to glow. It illuminated the inside of the room and he looked down into the garden.

"Fuck!"

He'd been drunk when he'd first seen the Black Lake Morris men. Now recognition seared into his being. The dirty, degenerating cloth of the baldrics, the grey once white shirts. Even the rusted bells at their shins. They stood over a collapsing man. The man was his father.

Forgetting his self-induced illness, Nathan bolted downstairs and into the lounge. He looked to the patio doors. His dad was flat on his back on the lawn. He leapt out of the door and across the grass.

Moggy's lips were blue, his eyes wide. He was trying to speak but was unable to form the words.

They were alone in the garden now. Nathan called his name again and again, tears springing from his eyes, not wanting to admit what he knew. Moggy's body slumped, free from agony now. He had gone.

Sixteen

Moth's real name was Maurice. He'd been christened Moth by the Wenley Morris Men not long after he's joined. The nickname had stuck. For years they had called him Moth and he'd never really thought about it until now, sitting here in his Land Rover in the middle of nowhere and miles from home. A sound made him turn, an engine noise.

The passing tractor pulling its high-sided metal trailer was a reminder for Maurice.

Dead by harvest's end.

Not that Maurice needed reminding. The shadow of the curse was over him. He could feel it every day. It was a certainty, as certain as summer. As certain as the harvest. He sat in the Land Rover staring at the spot where Graham had been killed. He'd parked the vehicle in a gateway shadowed by trees. He'd been here for hours.

Waking at dawn, Maurice left a message for Gerry at the workshop that he wouldn't be in today then had driven all the way down here to Oxfordshire to visit the place where it all started, the place where his friend of some thirty years had met his end. On the seat beside him the bunch of flowers lay. Bought from a garage on the M6. Graham wouldn't expect an Interflora bouquet, he knew that much. In the glove compartment was a bottle of Wenley Brewery Spite Eye. His favourite tipple.

Maurice had been staring at the spot for long enough, delaying the finality of the moment by laying the wreath.

"Fuck it," he said and pushed open the creaking door of the Land Rover. He grabbed the flowers and the bottle, and crossed the road to the place where Moggy's van had broken down all those weeks ago.

The bend in the road was innocuous looking, with pale blue tarmac, and weeds growing along the centre of the lane. A red-bordered triangular sign warning that there was a bend up ahead standing sentinel a few metres before him. There was no sign of the crash now. No broken bits of headlight or shattered bumper. No evidence that anything had happened here at all.

Maurice laid the flowers down on the bumpy grass verge and sat the bottle next to it. He stood for a moment at the edge of the road.

'Rest in peace, mate,' he said plainly, then walked away. A single tear rolled down his cheek at the thought of never seeing Graham again. He climbed into the car, defeated, and turned the ignition key.

The bugger didn't start.

"Come on you shit."

Frustrated, Maurice turned the key again, this time with force, but the vehicle just wouldn't kick into life. He got out, lifted the bonnet and fiddled with the wiring. Nothing seemed to be wrong. He tried starting it again but it just wouldn't take.

Maurice was stubborn enough not to own a mobile phone. Jan, his wife, had one but he'd never bothered. For the first time in his life, he wished he'd kept one in the glove compartment at least. He'd need to ring the RAC, and get a mechanic to look at it. The last thing he'd seen pass this way was that tractor and he'd not seen a single vehicle before or since.

The only house he'd noticed as he drove here was over the hill to the south. Maurice reckoned he could walk it from here. It hadn't looked too far. Besides, the owner of the house might know what this lane was called. It wasn't like a street where you could walk up the road and see the sign at the end. Even if he'd had a mobile, he still couldn't have told the RAC exactly where he was.

Some bloody lane outside of Bracewell, mate.

That wouldn't be much cop.

Maurice headed into the wood. Birds sang, warning of his approach as he followed a path through the sun-dappled foliage. He came to a stile and vaulted it, the footpath sigh pointing up to a meadow ahead then stopped dead.

Crowning the sign was a hat someone had left. A top hat ringed with drooping flowers of faded colour. A Morris man's hat.

He reached out for it, and swallowed hard. Finding this here was bloody strange. Someone could have left it from the day of dance but why would they? He could tell it had been left here recently. This was a sign. He knew it. He looked around to see if there was anyone watching. Maurice examined the hat once more then put it back.

That had freaked him out. Why leave something like that so close to where a Morris man died? It was odd. Sick, in fact. What's more how did they know he would be passing this way to find it? Maurice had the sudden awareness that he was meant to find it. That whoever had left that hat was part of the curse.

He quickened his step. He only had to cross another field to get to the farmhouse, he reckoned. Then he'd ask to use their phone. Maybe get a cup of coffee from them, maybe even breakfast. Right here, in this field the sanity of the normal world seemed very far away.

The slope inclined and he hurried to the next gate. He put his foot onto the middle rung of the rusted brown metal crossbar then found himself at the edge of a corn field. A corn field had been harvested. Mown yellow stubble stretched to the next gate and he could see the roof of the house beyond that. A large shape to his left caused him to start.

Parked adjacent to the edge a large yellow combine harvester faced him, its blade and octagonal gathering mechanism flat to the ground. The window of the cab blank, reflecting the morning sun.

Dead by harvest.

Movement on top of the beast caught his eye. They emerged, standing up as one so he got a good view, standing on the back of the harvester looking down. Five Morris men in kit, arms folded regarded him from above. Maurice knew at that instant that they weren't people. The dead faces, the features shadowed by their hats – the exact one he'd seen in the signpost – and the threatening stance they adopted told him they weren't friendly.

They were a threat, not a fellow Morris side he could have a friendly chat with. Every instinct told him to get away from them as fast as possible.

He stepped away from the combine harvester and stumbled across the field. Maurice dared to look back to see them still there. One sat down on top of the cab, another reclined across the back end. They looked like a gang, droogs from that old film he'd once seen, 'A Clockwork Orange'. At least they weren't following him but he was aware of their presence regarding him even when he turned his back.

The gate appeared to be miles away, just a tiny square in the distance but he quickened his pace, not wanting to break into a run, not wanting to show them his fear.

Who were they? It didn't make sense but at the same time it did. Were they ghosts? Spirits? Something to do with the curse?

Behind him, further down the field, the abrupt mechanical growl shattered the silence of the field.

The harvester had started up.

The accelerator was being pushed hard. Maurice dared a glance back, and saw a grey spume emerge from the upright exhaust pipe. The harvester mechanism lifted from the ground, the octagonal, spiky gathering mechanism, the auger, began to turn.

He ran, crying out. The harvester accelerated forwards, bouncing across the field at speed. He pelted onwards. The gate was getting closer but was still too far away.

Looking back, he glimpsed the figures riding on the back of the harvester, noted the shape of a man wearing a baldric behind the tinted glass of the cab. Maurice noted he was not wearing a hat. One of them was driving this thing.

He wasn't going to make it. He simply wasn't going to make it to the gate. The blade lowered and the thrash of the cutting blades started, the auger continued to turn ready to sweep him in.

Then it all stopped.

Silence.

Stillness.

Maurice looked around him to see that the scene had frozen. The harvester and its mechanisms no longer moved, and were silent. Even a flock of birds hung in midair. Everything had simply...stopped. He felt as if he were looking at a photograph.

"Moth."

Maurice turned. Graham stood there in his full Morris kit. With a clarity that he'd not ever felt before Maurice knew that he was dead. Graham had his hand out, an urgency in his voice.

"Come on, Moth. This way." Maurice moved towards him. "We've got work to do."

When he faced his friend, he noticed that Graham looked younger, in better health than he'd been in his life. In one hand he held an open bottle of Wenley Brewery's Spite Eye.

"Thanks, by the way," said Graham raising the bottle then taking a swig, "Bit early, I know, but what the heck? Come on, we've got important stuff to do."

"Like what?"

Behind him the scene began again. He turned to look. The harvester was moving, the birds continued their flight.

"No. Don't watch!" implored Graham. "Don't see how it ends."

Maurice watched in horror as he saw himself standing impassive as the harvester neared. He watched at the octagonal gatherer hooked into his body and delivered him into the cutting blades. He saw his flesh mangled, the blades grind and stop them they failed to bite through the thicker bones of his body.

***

In the baking afternoon sun, five Morris men approached the stile that Maurice had crossed to meet his end a few hours earlier. The lane was quiet as usual. Birds stopped singing in the trees at their approach, and even the breeze that rustled the upper branches of the trees seemed to die down.

One Morris man reached forwards and retrieved his hat from the footpath sign and placed it back on his head. Silently, they crossed the lane and disappeared into the trees, passing from solidity to shadow as they walked.

Seventeen

"I was expecting a visit from you," said Harris upon seeing who waited at the door step.

Without being asked Nathan crossed the threshold. Harris closed the door behind him.

Nathan had been to her place a few times. She lived with her parents in a huge Georgian house in Walton-on-Thames. He'd never seen her parents. Signs that they existed, at least her mother, were left almost strategically around the house. A double bass in its stand, crotchet books on the bookshelves, and a vase full of knitting needles on the windowsill.

Nathan went to the living room and dumped himself onto the low sofa. He'd only just got back from Leeds, where the family were preparing Moggy's funeral.

"Can I get you some herbal tea?" she said.

"Rather have something stronger," he said, "but I better not. I've been drinking a lot lately."

She returned minutes later with a cup of herbal tea and a handful of notes. She sat opposite him on the sofa, not speaking for some time, her thin legs curled under her. At last, she broke the silence.

"I can't imagine what you're going through."

He didn't look at her when she spoke. "I'm the last one. Maurice's gone missing somewhere and they don't know where he is. I know he's dead. This I all my fault. I brought this on us all."

He put his head in his hands and wept. Harris didn't come over. She sat there looking awkward, attempting to say something but then retracting any words of sympathy before she could speak.

"I never believed it", he said trying to compose himself. "The things I've seen since it happened. Fucking ironic. It's true. The curse is true."

"Well, I've been looking into the history of the Bracewell tradition since this started happening. I heard about the crash in Bracewell, then when Jake got murdered, I decided to dig deeper."

"I don't suppose you found a spell to revere the curse, did you? Dance the fucking thing forwards?"

"I'm afraid not. I did find out why Cecil Sharp destroyed all the Bracewell documents. He found out that it was cursed. 'Shepherd's Warning'. I went to my usual sources on Folk history: Pemberton, Evans, Hussein. They dug up news stories from local papers about other sides who had danced 'Shepherd's Warning' and died. In the late nineteenth century, a few sides danced it. One side's Squire was trampled by cows, another killed in a threshing accident. The stories didn't link the deaths to the dance but there is a pattern."

"Spare me the details."

"Not everybody who danced the dance died."

Nathan sat up. It felt like Harris had turned a light on in his mind.

"One of Cecil Sharp's academic contingent called Miles Sullivan danced the dance one May morning as a one-man jig. Pemberton had Sullivan's diary and it detailed how, as an atheist and rationalist, he wanted to prove that the curse was a myth. Just like you did. However, he writes that he felt an awful cloud of darkness over him afterwards and was gripped by terrible fear. He stopped writing his diary soon after but he did go back to Bracewell. Not to dance, but for some other reason he doesn't allude to in his diaries. He danced the dance in 1905 and was killed in action at The Somme in 1917. He didn't die before the harvest was out, that's for sure but he never wrote of how he broke the curse or why he returned to Bracewell."

"Anything else?"

"Nothing specific."

"Shit," he said taking a deep breath. "Well, what do you think? Do you think it's coincidence that all of the Morris men in my side died?"

"No. I keep an open mind on such things but this has prised my mind and my beliefs wider. That terrible cloud haunts me. It's called guilt. I should have never have found the dance for you. I'm undecided in what I believe, but I think there are forces in the word that direct our lives. If we mock them, they may just direct us to where we don't want to go."

"But there is a way to stop it. This Sullivan geezer managed it. Come on Harris, give me something else." He leaned towards her. "You said that you found out why Cecil Sharp burned all the Bracewell dances."

"Well, according to Hussain there is an account by his associate Mary Neale that, after dancing 'Shepherd's Warning' at Bracewell he became very disturbed. He told her he was being menaced by ghostly Morris men. He went back to Bracewell and these apparitions desisted. Sullivan returned to Bracewell, Sharp returned to Bracewell. Whatever the answer is, Nathan, it lays in Bracewell. You have to go back."

***

Back at the flat Nathan took the box down from the shelf. He removed the Webly, checked the mechanism and stored the bullets and the gun at the bottom of his bag. He slept in his clothes, the alarm set for six am to catch the first train to Oxfordshire.

Eighteen

The last time Nathan had been to Bracewell his father had picked him and Jake up in the truck. This time he'd have to find a way to get there on his own. Walking down the stairs into the entrance hall of the station a wave of grief hit him so hard he had to sit down for a few minutes.

He took his dad for granted, assumed he'd always be there. He knew Moggy would pass away but he vaguely envisioned this happening years into the future when Moggy was an old man, pissing himself in some care home. The reality was it had happened now. His funeral was days away.

He remembered the subdued excitement he and Jake felt stepping into this station a few weeks ago. Looking forwards to a weekend of drinking and dancing. He felt sick recalling his blind enthusiasm to dance the Dance of Death.

The wave of grief receded pulling the shade of memory from his mind and left him with another feeling. Anger. Maybe going to Bracewell would reveal to him the forces behind his friends and his father's deaths. Perhaps he would come face to face with the fuckers responsible for this. Maybe there was a way to get back at them, give them a fucking good kicking for what they'd done. He felt the weight of the gun in his hold all. Nathan didn't know what to expect when he went to Bracewell.

At the bus station the timetable just became a meaningless blur. In London and Leeds you got a tube or waited for a bus and there was always one in five minutes. The time was ten in the morning and the next bus to Bracewell wasn't until four in the afternoon.

Fuck that.

Nathan walked out of the town, past Banbury Cross and saw road signs for Adderbury – a famous Morris town – and Chipping Norton. He knew Bracewell was near to Hook Norton and west of the town so he walked along the road heading west out of Banbury. Overhead the grey sky glowered down. Was he actually going to walk to Bracewell? He didn't know how far it was but the first spots of rain were starting to fall.

He walked past old council houses, following the road. There was plenty of traffic so he assumed that this must still be the main road out of the town. The rain got heavier but as he rounded the corner, he could see a bend and an end to the buildings. This was the road out of town.

Nathan stopped by a large pub called The Easington, and waited under a tree. The rain was getting heavier, matching his mood. God this was depressing. He was alone in a strange place going to a village in the middle of nowhere to do, well, what?

He was tempted to turn back. Just go back to London, sit in the flat and wait his turn. No, screw that. He had to go to Bracewell but would get soaked if he walked there. He couldn't stay here. The watched the cars pass and an idea occurred to him. He stepped forwards and stuck out his thumb.

The cars were doing an average of 30mph here and if one did stop there was the pub entrance for them to pull into. Did people pick up hitch-hikers there days? He just didn't know. What if people thought he was s serial killer and they all drove past? What if a serial killer picked him up? Nathan had a comical image of himself fumbling around in the bag to get the gun between stabbing blows from his attacker.

After 40 minutes a pick-up truck stopped. A middle-aged man with a sheep dog riding next to him said he was actually going past Bracewell on his way to Hook Norton. The man didn't say much which was fine by Nathan; he wasn't feeling that chatty himself.

They turned off of the road into Bracewell and in a field to the left Nathan saw a police cordon around a lone combine harvester.

"What happened here?" asked Nathan.

"Some silly bugger walked into the path of a combine. Chewed him to bits. Poor bastard."

A new sick feeling dragged at Nathan's being. Could that had been Moth? His Land Rover had gone when he'd disappeared. Maybe he came here seeking answers too. Nathan couldn't cope with this new revelation so put his mind to the task ahead.

"This is as near as I can drop you," the farmer said.

"Thanks," he replied getting out. The pickup drove away and Nathan walked down the short lane to the village emerging past two houses onto the village green. He decided to try the pub first. As he crossed the village green couldn't help but notice the stone edifice of the church, darkened in the rain with the black clouds above and behind painting a grim picture.

Pubs in villages didn't open at eleven like city pubs. The Red Lion didn't open until six. Nathan had to talk to someone. Ask someone.

There were only two people he knew here. Simon Weaver and Wallace. Wallace had taught them the tune and had seemed keen to dance it but he was cantankerous old fucker. Nathan remembered Simon Weaver's haunted look that weekend. He'd caught Weaver looking at him strangely a few times that weekend and the more he thought about it now the clearer the realization that Weaver knew something about this became.

He had no idea where Weaver lived. There was no one to ask because the village was deserted. A sorry sight in the pissing rain. He waited by the pub for a few minutes until he saw a woman coming out of a cottage by the green with dog on a read. He rushed up to her and he asked where Simon

lead

Weaver lived. She pointed to number eleven, further along the green.

Nathan faced an old black wooden door set into an ironstone frame. The cottage was thatched, ancient and had that lived-in look. He banged the knocker three times and fully expected a wife or a kid to answer, to tell him that Weaver was at work and wouldn't be home till late or, worse, he was away on business. Nathan wondered what he'd do then. Just as he was weighing up his options, the door opened and Weaver himself answered. On seeing Nathan standing there, his face dropped. For long seconds Nathan was speechless. Weaver spoke first.

"You shouldn't have come here."

***

Weaver's house reminded him of Harris'. Shelves of books, faded throws over low, solid settees. A double bass and a saxophone on a stand in the corner.

"I warned you." Weaver took a bottle of Brandy from the shelf and poured them both one. "I read about the deaths. They found someone near Corn Lane killed by a combine harvester. I assume it's one of your lot. How many of you are left?"

"Just me."

"Just you? Fucking hell."

"You knew this was going to happen?"

"You danced the Dance of Death. What the fuck did you think was going to happen?"

"Yeah, well I didn't listen."

"Then I should have broken your legs. I bet you'd rather have broken legs than a dead Morris side. Maybe I should have tried harder. I saw the Black Lake men after you danced...I should have said something...I don't know."

Nathan did a double take. "You've seen them? These fucking ghosts?"

"Yes. It's not the first time I've seen the Black Lake Men. They appeared to me about five years ago. On May morning."

"What happened?"

"It's a long story."

Nathan took a sip of the brandy. He could feel it warming his belly. "Well, I've got till harvest is done for you to tell it."

"Then I better be quick. The combine harvesters are already out."

Nineteen

Simon poured them another drink and began his story. Nathan could tell he wasn't relishing this. Weaver was having trouble knowing where to start. Eventually he spoke.

"I used to be like you. I never believed in all the supernatural stuff. Then one morning I went for a walk on May Day, down to the woods by Black Lake and I saw them. They spoke to me. Not with words. With…well…a pair of rusted Morris bell pads. Bell pad's that I'd thrown into the river Wye ten years before. They had them. They showed them to me."

"I don't understand."

"You might have heard about how I went into the pub afterwards out of my mind. People still talk about it. It's a small community. I better explain what led up to my meeting with the Black Lake Morris men.

"I grew up with folk music, with the Morris. You know my mum and dad were in Weird Village, the folk/rock band from the sixties. They still have their annual festival over in Little Hidden."

Nathan knew it well. He'd been to The Little Hidden Festival of Music and Dance a few times, even seen Simon Weaver's dad, Bruce playing with his old bandmates.

"So, my dad helped revive the Bracewell Morris side in the Seventies. They danced Adderbury but never any of the Bracewell dances, even though Wallace knew them. Mum danced clog with Banbury Steppers. Me and my brother Callum knew no different. When I became a teenager, I began to get fed up with it when I got interested in girls and started to rebel. I was a pretty good dancer. Callum was better."

"I heard you gave it up to be a stockbroker or something."

"Not quite. It was Wallace that hammered the final nail in the coffin of my dancing. Back then he was Squire of the side. He was a perfectionist. You'd do a dance well and he'd pick you up on some small thing, a missed caper or a second too late getting back to your place after a hay. This was pretty irritating. We went down to the Forest of Dean for their weekend of dance. Do you know a pub there called The Boat? It's by the river Wye and built into the side of a hill. The road runs between the riverbank and the pub. I was going to dance a solo jig, 'Ladies of Pleasure'. From Bledington."

"Not that easy to dance," said Nathan. "I have problems with all those hook leg movements."

"Well, I cracked it. Callum had danced it the month before so all eyes were on me. There were other sides standing round watching and Wallace giving me the evil eye. Callum played the tune on his accordion. So, I danced it and got a huge round of applause from everyone. I'd managed to finish on the wrong foot. No one noticed and I remember thinking *great, that's over I can get a beer now.* As the applause died down Wallace stormed over and had a massive go at me. 'Left foot finish,' he actually screamed. 'Left foot!' I'd had months of this in our weekly practice. I just lost it. I told him he could shove Morris dancing up his arse. I tore off my bell pads and threw the in the river Wye. I remember hoiking my arm right up and they flew over everyone's heads and hit the water. The river Wye was wide at that point and deep. No one was going to get them back. I stormed off, went back to the campsite, packed up and went home. I hitch-hiked back to Bracewell. I was done with Morris dancing for good."

"So, what brought you back?"

He drained his brandy and exhaled. "Fear. Fear brought me back."

"That's an odd thing to say."

"I know. I left Bracewell when I was eighteen. Went to uni, got a job, lived in London. Callum stayed here and continued as Squire of the Bracewell side. I worked in IT sales and went all over the world. I became quite materialistic. Wore a suit, drove an Audi. My dad was horrified that I'd become a yuppie. Then Callum became ill. He got lung cancer which metastasised to the brain. Mum and dad were getting older and couldn't cope with looking after Callum, so I came home to help. One night, when Callum was feeling a bit stronger, we went to the pub. He asked me to dance at his funeral, asked me to dance 'Vandals of Hammerwich' with the rest of the side. I said no. The thought of putting on all that clobber, doing those dances…I dunno…I'd moved on. That was the last time we went out. He became iller then. He asked me again and again I refused. Dad knew he wanted me to dance at this funeral and leaned on me quite heavily. Wallace cornered me one evening in the pub and told me to dance at Callum's funeral. I told him to fuck off. He must have known something because he said, and I remembered this clearly, if I didn't there would be consequences. I just thought he was mad. A couple of strange things happened. One morning I opened the lounge windows and a Morris stick had been stuck in the ground and a battered looking hat with dead flowers left on top of it. I accused Wallace of doing this but he denied it.

"Callum got worse. To make up for not dancing at this funeral I tried to become the model brother and son to Mum and Dad. I got a hospital bed, hired a private nurse to care for him twenty-four hours a day. In the April his observations became dangerously low. His blood oxygen levels were low, blood pressure was also low. He was dying. Mum and Dad and me sat round his bed. He was murmuring and mumbling but was so out of it on morphine by then to make

121

sense. He died in the room upstairs. The nurse took his pulse and it wasn't there anymore. He'd stopped breathing.

"The moment he died, or as near as damn it, we heard a noise from the wardrobe. A clatter and a thump. Something had fallen down in there but it had made such a noise we had to look. I opened the door and his Morris kit was on the floor. The bells and the baldric were on the floor like someone had pulled them off of the hanger. It was like he was trying to tell me one more time to dance at his funeral.

"Mum and Dad went away and I arranged the funeral. It was due to take place a couple of days after May Day. You know what May Day is like here. People turn up from all over the county. I didn't want to be part of it so I got up in the middle of the night and just walked. I found myself down by the lake. I was alone in the wood and sensed someone following me. So, I got out of the wood. That's when I saw them. Face to face. In the field behind the church. They surrounded me. They were ghosts, dead men walking, their faces…one of them held up something. My bells that's I'd chucked in the river years before. They had them in their hands. How the fuck they'd got hold of them I'll never know. Callum wanted me to dance at his funeral, so did Dad, so did Wallace, and so did the Black Lake Morris men."

"So, you danced at his funeral."

"They shocked me out of my petulant hate for the Morris. I did 'Vandals of Hammerwich' as he requested."

122

"Then you stayed and took Callum's place. You could have left."

"I should have. Mum and Dad were in bits. They eventually moved to Spain and I got this house and fell into the routine of village life again. You see, I got the feeling they wanted me to stay. The handing back of the bells was symbolic. They wanted me to take Callum's place, rejoin the side, organize the annual weekend of Dance here. They terrified me that morning. I thought, if they can find my bells, they can find me. I never wanted to see them again. My mind nearly flipped the first time. I do all this to keep them away. After a while it becomes routine, you don't think about it. And I learned to live with it, even enjoyed it all again but then you turn up. You turn up with that fucking dance and, ta da, I *see* them again. Tell me, Nathan, do you understand now? All your friends dying, has that finally opened your eyes."

"Yes," Nathan said quietly.

"Then you'll know you can do nothing about it. You just have to accept your fate."

Nathan glared at him. "Bullshit. I'm not going to sit around and wait to die. Yes, I'm frightened of those fucking lake zombies, but I'm more frightened of dying. The curse can be undone. I just need to find out how."

Twenty

Nathan told him about Sullivan, the man Harris had read about and who had, supposedly, reversed the curse.

Nathan had slept in the spare room until ten. Simon cooked him a full English and he realised that he'd not eaten properly for days. They sat opposite each other on the breakfast bar tucking into the food.

"Wallace knows all about this," Simon stated, his words hitting the silence with flat certainty.

Nathan laughed darkly. "Huh…he was next on my list to visit."

"Why didn't you go and see him first?"

"Because I don't trust the fucker. Do you think he knew this would happen?"

"I don't know. When I'd had my encounter, I danced at Callum's funeral. Afterwards, at the wake, he came up to me and said 'See, if the Morris men want something, they gets it.'"

"That's a pretty accurate impression of him."

"Thank you. It was only afterwards that I realised what he meant. He didn't mean Morris men in general. He meant

124

The Morris men. The Bracewell Lake Morris Men. I never liked him. After I chucked my bells in the river and told him where to shove it, we really didn't have much to say to each other, even after I came back to the Morris."

"Shit. It's like a fucking ghost mafia. But they never bothered you again."

"They never bothered me. The next time I saw them was the weekend you came. You danced 'Shepherd's Warning' and they were in the graveyard, watching."

Nathan and Simon both knew their next step but only Simon was brave enough to say it out loud once they'd finished eating.

"We're going to have to go and see him."

"I know." Nathan sat back. "It just feels like going to get help from Satan himself, you know."

"We only have to talk to him. If we make it clear were not here to fuck about, we might get some straight answers from him."

"And if we don't?"

He shrugged. "We could call the vicar. I spoke to her after my encounter and she was all up for going down to the lake and performing an exorcism. I declined. I didn't want to start a war between the lake men and the church." Simon stood up. "Come on. It's noon. He'll be digging his garden. We can catch him at his house."

"I need a piss first. It's that coffee."

Nathan felt something close to optimism for the first time. In the bathroom he admired the gold and platinum discs from sixties and seventies Weird Village albums that Simon's parents had made. At any other time, he would have been wowed, but with everything that had gone on his grief had taken the edge off the moment.

Simon was waiting for him at the door. They exited into the fresh air. Wisps of clouds blew through the sky as they crossed the green. Sunlight punctuated the ground creating shadows that flickered on and off.

At Wallace's cottage, Nathan remembered the day he'd visited with Wojtek, Jake and the others. It now seemed so long ago but the place was fresh in his mind. Nathan tried to counter this cognitive loosening by focusing on the task ahead.

Nathan expected Simon to knock on the front door. Instead, he walked into the side passage.

"Aren't we supposed to knock?'

"That would be the polite thing to do,' agreed Simon, 'but fuck him. I don't waste politeness on people I don't like."

Nathan wanted to laugh. He was beginning to like Simon. He could imagine him as a no-bullshit sales negotiator driving a BMW. He wondered how rude he would be to his old Squire.

Wallace was digging the garden. They watched as the old man in stained nylon trousers cut off at the knee tried with

tied

a bit of string heaved clumps of dirt out of the ground with his fork. Nathan wondering how to open the dialogue when, without looking, he addressed them.

"Thought you would have been here earlier. After the first one wot got killed." He turned and almost smirked at Nathan. "Bit slow to twig, were yer? You knew the stories. Thought you'd have worked it out."

"If you knew then why the fuck did you teach us the dance? Why the fuck did you give us the music?"

Nathan took an aggressive step forward. Wallace raised the fork and openly laughed.

"It weren't down to me. I was just doing what I was told. And you don't say no to the Lake men, do you Simon?"

Simon didn't reply, just glowered.

"So, you know them? The Lake Men?"

Wallace stabbed the fork into the ground and fumbled in his pocket. He pulled out a twenty-pound note. He held it out to Simon. "Here. Go down the shop and half a dozen bottles of Hooky beer. Bring 'em back here. Me and the lad are going to sit down," he gestured to an old deckchair and a rusting beer barrel at the bottom of the overgrown garden, "and I'm gonna tell him how he can get rid of this curse."

Twenty-One

"So how many Morris men did you see that night in the woods?"

"I can't remember," said Nathan. "I was pissed. Five I think."

"You ask Master Weaver when he gets back how many he saw that day and he'll tell you. Five. Most dances in the Morris are for six men. There's the odd one like Vandals of Hammerwich and some other Lichfield dances which is for eight, but six is the number. The world was made in six days. The mark of the beast is three sixes. The Lake boys wants a sixth man to dance with them. That's all. That's why they was so interested in watching you dance 'Shepherd's Warning'. They knew there would be another man to dance with them in the afterwards. Sixth man to dance with them on the lake of a May Day."

"Listen. A friend of mine found a historical document where a man who'd danced 'Shepherd's Warning' came back to Bracewell and did something to remove the curse."

"Miles Sullivan." Wallace grinned knowingly.

"You know about this?"

"I knows about everything. My dad told me about Sullivan, and it was my dad what told Sullivan how to get rid of the curse. It weren't long after the Lake boys died. He danced it as a jig. Stupid bugger."

"Then how did he stop the fucking curse?"

Wallace sniffed and shuffled his backside in the deck chair, the old thing threatening to swallow him up.

"Dying ain't no big thing to them as is dead. No more than crossing the bridge to Wake's meadow. The power of the curse come from the other side. Where the Lake boys is now. The Lake boys can come back into this world somehow. Sullivan petitioned the Lake boys to go back into the other side and, in turn, petition them who makes the curse work."

"Okay, but what did he actually do, for fuck's sake? Sacrifice a goat? Read the Bible backwards? Piss into and upside-down pentagram, what?"

Nathan was becoming more than irritated by Wallace's casual nature.

"Sullivan petitioned them. Another way of puttin' it is he asked them nicely. He went up to the wood at dusk and spoke to them. My dad showed him how."

Here was a glimmer of light. If Wallace's dad knew how to do this then he should be able to as well. However, he could imagine the old bastard refusing just to be cussed or dragging his heels, taking pleasure in seeing Nathan sweat.

If he did any of this Nathan would brain the fucker. He could feel his fists clenching.

"Twilight. That's the time to go up to the woods. We'll go up there then."

The gate squeaked and Simon returned with a plastic bag bulging with beer bottles.

Nathan stood. "I need a drink."

"They're not for you," said Wallace. "They're for the Lake Morris Men. An offering." He stood up. "Just going inside for a widdle. Don't go drinkin' them beers."

As soon as Wallace was out of sight Simon turned to him. "And?"

"He wants me to go up to the woods with him this evening. At dusk."

"I take it I'm not invited."

Nathan frowned. "I guess not."

"Yeah, well. I'll be right behind you. Out of sight. I don't trust him. Not one bit."

Twenty-Two

"Right. Better be off then."

Wallace stood up and Nathan swilled down the awful cup of tea that had been made for him. Nathan had gone back to Simon's house to talk with him some more. They tried to reason how these supernatural entities operated until the sun began to sink over the horizon. Palms sweaty with anticipation Nathan returned to Wallace's cottage.

Simon had promised to follow at the distance once they'd left Wallace's. Nathan didn't want to arouse Wallace's suspicions by actively looking for him.

Wallace had made a show of hospitality on Nathan's return and made a pot of tea. Begrudgingly, Nathan had taken up the offer of a cup. Wallace seemed exited to be going into the woods like they were going on a camping trip or something.

Nathan picked up the bottles of beer in their carrier bag and made his way to the door.

Before they left put a friendly hand on Nathan's shoulder. "It's going to be all right, son. It's going to be all right."

The man's features seemed to soften and Nathan felt, for the first time, that maybe Wallace could be trusted after all and was genuinely trying to help.

They headed up the hill to the barn and small field where they'd camped a few weeks ago. Nathan was glad to see Simon in the corner of his eye, darting across the road behind them.

***

Simon could hear Wallace whistling and saw them enter the woods from just behind the barn. He skipped across the small field and crossed the gate into the woods following the footpath that they'd taken. Simon reasoned that if he turned left and went into the field, he could cut them off. He could enter the wood further along where the stile crossed into the wood, the one he'd used all those years ago, when he'd first seen the Lake Men.

He crashed through the under growth – Nathan and Wallace were too far ahead to hear his elephantine efforts, he hoped – and jumped the barbed wire fence into the field. A group of Jersey cows at the top of the hill gave him a curious glance but went back to munching their grass. The dying rays of the sun reddened the tops of the trees behind him and cast the grass into shadow. From here he could see the stile further down the hill and ran for it.

Beyond the wooden FOOTPATH sign and the stile, the wood was in darkness but he could just about make out a man's shape. As he neared the figure stepped out and through the wood of the stile, as the Lake Morris men had done all those years ago. The apparition blocked his path.

No. It can't be.

Simon was faced with a Morris man in the Bracewell kit. Red Baldric and hat garlanded with flowers. However, he wasn't decayed and his kit was clean, his whites bright.

"This is no business of yours, Simon. You must go back. Leave them to it." The man spoke with a clear, voice that Simon recognised immediately.

He looked into the face of the young man and said his name.

"Callum."

Twenty-three

The twilight was beginning to have a strange effect on Nathan. He felt a growing, nagging fear in his mind. He sat on the ground by the lake and Wallace perched on a log. Before them, the five opened bottles of Hooky ale sat on the bank like bait intended to lure in some waterborne alcoholic. Ghost bait, thought Nathan.

What the hell was he doing here with this old man in a wood at dusk? It didn't make sense, but then again nothing that had happened since first visiting this place back in June did. The weird caffeine feeling continued followed by a muscular sluggishness. Maybe his body was tired but his mind wasn't. It had been a long day after all. He wondered of Weaver being here, hiding nearby no doubt, might prevent them from appearing.

"They aren't coming," Nathan said flatly.

"They will. Just give it time." Wallace took another puff on his pipe. "So, tell me. What's your favourite dance to do?"

"I dunno. 'The Upton on Severn Stick Dance'. That's fun to do. Some of the border dances can be a good laugh."

"But there's nothing like it, is there? When you've got a good audience and you've got a good side to dance with. When you're doing it, when you're totally focused on the stepping and the figures. There's nothing like it in the world is there? Six men dancing as one. The world don't matter, you have no cares right in those moments. Am I right?"

Nathan thought about it. Wallace was right. It wasn't just the beer and the chance to spend some time in a pretty village or whatever. When they danced, they were totally focused on the movements. Flow, psychologists called it. When your mind is so into what you're doing that you're totally content for that moment. He often felt it playing in the band. And afterwards the feeling of satisfaction, of a job well done was sometimes euphoric. Well, he wouldn't be dancing with his side any more. Those days were over. He could find another side to dance with but after this he wasn't sure he wanted to carry on with it.

"Course," Wallace continued. "I can't dance no more. My knees is buggered but you got years left in you. Centuries even."

Nathan looked up at him. Why did he say that?

"Those boys what danced on the lake back in eighteen ninety. They was like you. Well, in a lot of ways they was and in a lot of ways they weren't. They was farm labourers. Ploughboys. Woodcutters. All they wanted to do was dance."

"And it killed them. They drowned when the ice cracked."

"And a gift was give to them."

"What do you mean?" Nathan really was feeling sluggish now. Like his muscles just wanted to go to sleep but his brain wouldn't let them.

"Why do you think you're here? By chance? How do you think you got to be in Bracewell in the first place?"

"We came here for the weekend of dance."

"Yes. That was set up by Simon Weaver. Now he turned his back on the Morris years ago. I was there when he chucked his bells in the river. Good set of bells they was too. He'd be gent in the city now or living abroad again if it weren't for the Lake Men. They visited him that morning because they wanted him back in the Morris."

The conversation he'd had with Simon about his fear of the Lake Men came back to him.

"He danced at his brother's funeral. Then he stayed. He re-joined the side, set up the day of dance. The Lake Men knew he would do this. The Lake Men they seen everything in Bracewell and beyond. They knew you was a good dancer. They had their eye of you. They wanted you to Dance 'Shepherd's Warning', start the curse."

"Fuck off, Wallace. It doesn't work like that. They don't control reality."

"No. You're right but they needs us to do their work for them. It was me what gave the dance to your mate Harris.

136

They told me to, to lure you in. And you came to Bracewell. And I gave you the tune and showed you the stepping. I even played it for you on the day you danced. See?"

"Fucking…what? You knew Harris?"

"Her Oxford contact. That was me. And when you danced the dance, the curse began. The Lake Men was watching. They knew eventually you'd come back here to try and save yourself."

He shot to his feet, felt woozy and steadied himself on a tree. "This is a set up? Why? For fuck's sake?"

"Because, like you said, nothing is better than dancing. And the Lake Men they gets to do it forever. Thing is, there's only five of them and, as you know, most dances are done with six. They need one more man."

"But, my side: Wojtek, Maurice. They could have chosen from one of them."

"They died so you'd come here. They wanted the best dancer in the country and that, my friend is you. They wants you to dance with them."

The truth began to dawn on Nathan. The Lake Men wanted Nathan dead. They wanted him dead to dance with them. The other thing he realised was that Wallace had drugged him.

As if reading his mind the old man said, "There's a fungus what grows in these woods. I been taking it for years. Helps me sleep. Slip a little in me tea pot and I goes off like a light. You ain't used to it so it works better with you.

137

Listen. To join the Lake Men you has to drown in their water. Them's the rules. Now, you is a big lad. I couldn't get you in there me self but like this you is as weak as a baby."

To prove the point, he pushed Nathan back and let him stumble against a tree. Nathan aimed a punch and his slow, flailing arm went wide. Wallace grinned.

"It don't take long to drown. A few gulps, yer lungs fills up then it's all night night. You'll be dancing before you can say…well…before you can say 'Shepherd's Warning'."

"Simon," he yelled. "Simon, the fucker's drugged me."

Like in a dream his yells came out as low groans.

Laughing, Wallace went behind him and pushed him. Nathan stumbled forwards towards the water. His vision was blurry but he could see five figures standing waist heigh in water. Their arms outstretched in greeting.

Inside his jacket pocket he reached for the gun but Wallace plucked it out of his hand and threw it onto the grass. Wallace pushed him forwards again and Nathan teetered on the edge of the bank. The black, dark water was waiting for him.

"What yer waiting for? Christmas?" Wallace laughed and pushed him from behind. "Or May Day?"

Nathan tried to go sideways and knocked over the bottles of beer set there. He felt two strong hands push from behind and he hit the water.

Twenty-Four

Nathan tried to move his limbs to swim but they simply wouldn't work. The lake couldn't have been that deep, surely. He couldn't feel the bottom and wondered if his nerves were registering any feeling down there. Wallace's fungus tea had really done its work.

Blind panic made Nathan struggle harder. His head went under and he took in a mouthful of dirty tasting brackish water. He surfaced and could still see the Morris men standing there, waiting for him to die.

To die.

Maybe he should just give in. Get it over with. People said that when you drown, after the struggle it becomes like a dream. He wondered how they knew.

Don't give up son.

A voice came clear in his mind. Moggy's voice. His dad. He really was hallucinating now. Hallucination or not, he struggled even harder to stay alive, and his hand hit something. A tree root sticking out onto the water. His hands seemed to work better than his legs and he gripped it, and began to pull. Nathan was aware of figures in the water closing it. The Lake Men. They weren't going to let him go. Where the hell was Weaver? Surely, he should have seen what was going on by now. Wallace couldn't have overpowered him.

Exhausted, Nathan's grip on the branch loosened and he felt himself sinking into the water. He felt himself descending into the dark. All he had to do was to take in one lungful of water and he'd be dancing with the Lake Men, free from suffering, drowning all done.

As he began to let himself float down, a pair of strong hands gripped Nathan's shoulders and heaved him clear out of the water.

Like a spluttering newborn infant, he emerged into the air and hit the ground. Nathan lay there, his hands working but his legs still numb from the fungus tea. A familiar face filled his vision, and he felt hands on his back helping him to sit. Nathan expected to see Weaver but confusion soon crept over his face as he looked up to see his dad standing over him.

Moggy still had the beard but looked somehow younger, his blue eyes burned with a mischievous light. Nathan shook his head and climbed to his feet. He was surrounded by the other Morris men: Wojtek, Jake, Maurice and Graham. They were all in kit, their whites almost glowing. Behind them he could see more Morris men and women in different kits and old farm clothes.

"Am I dead?" he asked Moggy.

Moggy laughed. "No son. It's nowhere near your time yet. You got pretty close through."

To his left the Lake Men were standing on the water like unholy apparitions. They regarded the scene on the bank with their usual glowering disdain. Wojtek bent down and picked up one of the bottles of beer and drank deep.

From the lake one of the Morris men spoke, his voice like a death growl.

"That...was left...for us."

"Fuck you," spat Wojtek. "Fuck you and go fuck your mother. You took my life I take your fucking beer. *Mash piwor. kurwa, pizzda...*"

"Wojtek," snapped Moggy, "shut it." He stood on the bank and faced the Lake Men. "You boys have a lot to answer for. There's folks here who want a bloody word with you but that can wait. Now, I tried to reason with you. Tried to offer myself as your sixth dancer but you ignored me and still went ahead and tried to take my son. You've crossed the line there, pal. Crossed the bloody line. Now, you want someone to dance with you. I offer myself. I've been dancing all my life and can keep up with you any day. What do you say?"

"We...want...your...son."

"You're not fucking getting him! What did I tell you? I'm sorry you did something stupid over a hundred years ago and all got drowned but that's no reason to take it out on other people. Nathan's time is not at hand. That is bloody

141

written. Why do you think we're here? Now you take me or face the consequences."

Behind Nathan the crowd of ghosts closed in. He could see missing limbs, facial gashes. He realised that these people had all danced 'Shepherd's Warning' and met their end at the dead hands of the Lake Men.

Nathan saw the Lake Men shift uncomfortably on the water. They regarded each other.

"We…" the speaker paused and Nathan felt the temperature drop, *"…agree…"*

All around him the foliage began to turn brown, leaves curled in on themselves as they died. The grass paled and yellowed. Autumn had arrived in a heartbeat. The leaves fell to the ground almost as one and ice spread out across the lake like a rapid infection.

Moggy turned to Nathan and put his hands on his shoulders.

"The curse is over son. These men have got what they want." Moggy hugged his son. "I love you Nathan. Live a long life. Look after your mum. And keep dancing. Don't let this put you off. Teach your kids to dance, do it till your knees give out and even then, carry on. It's a short life and we'll meet again. Take care son. You best leave now."

The other guys moved forwards and they shook hands. Jake met his eyes but didn't speak, just grinned sadly.

I like
·
Singly

142

The glade was covered with ice and the lake was frozen solid just like it must have been when the Lake Men met their end.

"Right, what we dancing?" said Moggy stepping onto the ice.

"*Shepherd's... Warning...*" growled the dancer.

"Shepherd's bloody Warning. What else?"

"Can I watch?" asked Nathan.

"No," snapped Moggy taking his place at the front of the set, the six of them now lined up ready to dance. "You've seen enough. This is not meant for the eyes of the living."

A woman in a bonnet and shawl carrying an according *accordion* passed right through him. Followed by a guy with a white beard wearing a bowler hat and brightly decorated waistcoat carrying a viola. They took their instruments, ready to play.

Nathan really felt that he should leave and as the minor chords of the music for 'Shepherd's Warning' began an acute nausea came over him. The music carried a grim tone that made the death metal he played with Innocent Souls sound like a jolly radio jingle. It really was time to leave.

Amid the frost on the ground, he saw the Webley. Before he left the glade Nathan scooped it up and stuffed it into his jacket.

Twenty-Five

The village sat in darkness. Across the green Nathan could see a faint light burning in Simon Weaver's house. He waited in the shadow of the old man's cottage. This side of the road was a quiet as the grave. Nathan broke that silence when he booted the front door open and stormed in.

Wallace was struggling out of his low settee chair when Nathan barged into the living room. The look of incomprehension in his eyes on seeing the sacrifice still alive was pure gold as far as Nathan was concerned. He raised the gun and pointed it right at his face. He stood there for long minutes, his finger on the trigger.

"Go on then. Do it!" spoke the old man at last.

Nathan stood, hand steady, eyes fixed. Wallace swallowed hard.

"I'm ready," snarled Wallace.

Nathan lowered the gun and pointed it his crotch.

"What are you doing? No!"

"I'm not going to kill you," said Nathan, "I'm going to cripple you. Shoot you in the hips. Disable you. It'll hurt and you gardening days will be over. How about that?"

"For God's sake man, have some pity."

Nathan launched forwards, jammed the gun into the old man's mouth. "You tried to kill me, you old fuck. Drugged me and tried to drown me. Give me one reason why I should let you live? Eh?"

Nathan saw the terror in his eyes. He withdrew the gun and stood up.

"It's over. I just wanted you to feel fear. Feel what it was like. You're old Wallace. You'll die soon and when you do you'll pay for all the shit you've done."

Nathan threw the gun into the old man's lap. Wallace seized the weapon and pulled the trigger aiming at Nathan's crotch. It clicked uselessly in his hand. Nathan took the bullets from his pocket.

"Like I said, I just wanted to see the fear in your eyes."

"They won't take this laying down you know. They won't forget."

"And they won't forget you failed them, either."

Without thinking he left the bullets on the table before exiting the cottage.

***

Simon sat clutching a whiskey staring into the fire. Nathan entered the house without knocking. Simon poured him a glass and Nathan downed it in one. The cottage was utterly silent apart from the ticking of the grandfather clock.

"What happened to you?" Nathan almost snarled. "I nearly…never mind. Are you okay?"

"I saw my dead brother. I spoke to him."

"Well, there's a fucking coincidence. I saw my dead dad."

From across the green a single sharp shot from a gun shattered the silence of the village. Both men looked out of the window in the direction of Wallace's cottage.

***

Wallace loaded the bullet into the sliding mechanism and it fitted in with a click. He looked up at the five figures standing over him. Their bells rusted, their baldrics faded.

"Please. I…"

They didn't reply. He had failed them and knew what was required of him. If he hesitated, he'd not be able to go through with it and his crossing would be much worse. He put the barrel into his mouth as instructed and pulled the trigger.

Bracewell

May Day

Twenty Years Later

She led the set into the middle of the road. The early crowds were there looking on as the side began to dance.

Nathan held the baby sleeping in his arms and looked to his wife. Michelle Harris was grinning inanely as their gobby, sixteen-year-old daughter led the Bracewell Junior Morris Side into their first dance. 'Banbury Bill', from Ducklington.

Cally was exactly like her father: arrogant, strong-willed and determined. Since she'd been able to speak, she had argued with him but she'd picked up his talent for Morris dancing along the way too.

Now Nathan was in his forties and was certainly feeling it, especially since the arrival of their second unexpected child. He'd had to take a bit of a back seat when it came to dancing, but Cally carried it on.

Nathan looked over at Wallace's cottage. Now it was refurbished with a shiny new door and a gravel garden. He and Simon had found Wallace dead in his armchair after hearing the shot. Simon wasn't surprised but Nathan had been. He'd not told Simon about his conversation with Wallace, but he knew death was not the old man's intent. Nathan wondered what had prompted him to leave the bullets. Wallace had been more likely to load the gun and follow him across the green to finish Nathan off.

He shuddered.

Moggy had dealt with the Lake Men, surely. They were surrounded by very pissed off ghosts last time he'd been here. There was no way they would come back.

He'd not been here since that night. Simon had driven him to the station and he'd returned to London and got on with his life. He'd started a relationship with Harris, or Michelle as she was now to him; as his wife he felt obliged to call her by her first name. They'd had Cally and existed as a family of three for a good while, then last year Michelle had announced she was pregnant.

He swelled with pride at Cally's perfect stepping and spot on timing.

He'd not seen Weaver since that day. The pub had closed down and was now a house but he couldn't see him in the crowd. Maybe he'd moved out. He'd said he'd started the Morris again because he was afraid of them. Once their power was broken then maybe he'd fled?

Nathan was aware that he was being stared at, he felt it in his peripheral vision. He turned. Up the slope by the church, an old man in a Baldric and white shirt was staring at him. The old man lifted his hat and doffed it. Below Cally and the side had finished her dance.

Wallace.

Behind him the Lake Men fanned out. He saw them fully before they all faded from sight.

No. this was not possible. This was not happening.

Cally finished her dance and her confidence oozed from every pore. Her bright red hair shone in the early sun as she strutted around. Nathan knew, just knew, what was next. The Lake Men had waited. They'd played the long game. They'd waited for him to have kids before they positioned and nudged everything into place. Moggy hadn't stopped them. They were still powerful, and still active.

Cally called out in her loud voice and announced the next dance. Nathan wanted to rush forwards and stop them but his legs wouldn't move, his voice wouldn't work. In his head he was screaming "No!"

"Ladies and gentlemen. We would like to dance our next dance. This had not been danced in England for 20 years. 'Shepherd's Warning'. From Bracewell."

Acknowledgements

Morris dancing; national Joke or quant historical tradition? Whatever the answer, I feel I need to give thanks to the following groups and individuals who have directly or inadvertently helped me to shape *Shepherd's Warning* into a full-blown story.

Firstly, I'd like to thank my own Cotswold Morris side, Northampton Morris. I've been dancing with these guys for 10 years. Without their experience and expertise, the story would have lacked the kind of authenticity that I was aiming for. Thanks go to Squire Ian Phillips for taking me through the historical archives of the side, particularly for showing me the fantastically named 'Black Book' which contains outlines of the dances mentioned in the story. Thanks to all the other guys who answered questions, gave me feedback and debated if a "half gip" should be capitalised or not.

I also need to thank Rose and Castle Morris for clog-based shenanigans and adding fuel to the inspirational fire.

Acknowledgement needs to be made to the great Northampton Science Fiction Writers Group who workshopped the first few chapters and gave important advice and pointers on what to keep in and what to leave out. Thes guys have been a source of vital advice and encouragement for 20 years now.

Thanks also to Tim C. Taylor for deep, alcohol fuelled chats we had about writing and how to get ideas down.

Finally, a very special mention to my wife, Natalia. I hope this one keeps up you till 6 am like *High Cross* did. Love you.

Paul Melhuish,
Northamptonshire,
November 2023

Paul Melhuish is a 53-year-old Morris dancer who writes in his spare time. His previous novels include *Dark Choir* (published by Silver Shamrock Press in 2020) and *High Cross* (published by Horrific Tales in 2018). He has had other short pieces published in magazines and anthologies in Britian and the US and is a member of the Northampton Science Fiction Writers Group.

Find Paul online:
Website: paulmelhuish.wordpress.com
Facebook: @paul.melhuish.14

Printed in Great Britain
by Amazon

49909534R00091